Legacy of the Jedi

JEDI APPRENTICE

JEDI QUEST

Legacy of the Jedi

JUDE WATSON

SCHOLASTIC INC.

New York   Toronto   London   Auckland   Sydney
Mexico City   New Delhi   Hong Kong   Buenos Aires

www.starwars.com
www.scholastic.com

ISBN 0-439-53666-9

12 11 10 9 8 7 6 5 4 3 2 1   3 4 5 6 7 8/0

Printed in the U.S.A.
First printing, August 2003

CHAPTER No. 1

The corridor was empty. The two thirteen-year-old boys paused outside the closed door. There were locks at the Jedi Temple, but they were rarely used. There was no need. There was nothing to hide. Nothing was forbidden. The Jedi's code of honor gave each individual the challenge and privilege of walking the Jedi path. It was assumed that the discipline needed for this would also prevail in one's private life.

So to enter another Jedi's room without an invitation would not violate a rule. Not one that needed to be spoken or written, at least. Yet Dooku knew it was wrong. It wasn't *terribly* wrong. But it was wrong.

"Come on," Lorian said. "No one will find out."

Dooku glanced at his friend. Lorian's face was eager. A dusting of freckles scattered across his blunt nose like a dense constellation of stars. His eyes were warm, lit with mischief, a dark piney green with amber lights, like a forest shot with sunlight. Lorian had been suggesting schemes since they were seven, and he'd talked Dooku into exploring the garbage tunnels. The experience had left Dooku with a reeking tunic and a healthy respect for sanitation practices.

"Besides, he's your Master," Lorian said. "He wouldn't mind."

It was true that Thame Cerulian was Dooku's Master. The renowned Jedi Knight had chosen him last week. Dooku had just turned thirteen, and he was relieved that he wouldn't have to wait any longer to become a Padawan Learner. Yet he had not had time to get to know Thame at all. Thame was in the Outer Rim completing one last mission before taking on a Padawan. Dooku was proud to have been chosen by such a legend.

The question was, could he live up to that legend?

Dooku had to. Getting a peek into Thame's personal quarters might give him a head start.

He nodded at Lorian and accessed the door. It slid open silently. He stepped inside. If he expected a clue to his new Master's inner character, he was disappointed. The sleep couch was narrow, pushed against one wall. A gray coverlet was folded neatly at the bottom. A datascreen sat on a bare table. No laserprints or holograms hung on the wall. No personal items were on the desk or the small table beside the sleep couch. There was a glass carafe with a small glass stopper. The transparent vessel and the gray blanket were the only signs that someone actually inhabited the room.

"Wait," Lorian said. "I found something."

He slid his hands along a seam in the wall that was almost invisible. He pressed a recessed button and the wall slid back to reveal shelves over the desk. They were filled with holobooks.

Dooku bent to examine the titles. Thame, he knew, was a historian, an expert in Jedi history. He had never seen most of these titles before. Galactic history, biographies, the natural sciences of different atmospheres and planetary systems. It was an impressive library.

Lorian dismissed them with a glance. "You'd think he'd have had enough of studies after Temple training. I can't wait to get out into the galaxy and do things."

Dooku reached for a holobook with no title or author. He flipped it open and scanned a page.

Meditation beforehand is necessary in order to ready the mind. Some suffer from nausea or dizziness at first viewing. But primarily one must prepare for the effect of the dark side upon the mind, especially the young or weak. Nightmares and dark visions can result, lasting years. . . .

"This is a manual about the Sith Holocron," Dooku said, his voice a whisper now. He handled the holobook carefully.

"The Sith Holocron? But no one can view it," Lorian said.

"That's not so. Jedi Masters are allowed. Not many are interested. Most Jedi Knights think the Sith are extinct and will never return. Except for my Master." Dooku gazed at the book. His stomach twisted, as though he'd gazed upon the Sith Holocron itself. "He believes there will come a time when the Jedi will have to fight the Sith again."

"Does this manual tell you how to access the Holocron?" Lorian asked, interested now.

Dooku flipped through it, his heart beating. "Yes. It gives warnings and instructions."

"This is so galactic," Lorian murmured. "With the help of this handbook, we could access the Sith Holocron ourselves!" He looked at Dooku, his eyes shining. "We'd be the first Jedi Padawans to do it!"

"We can't!" Dooku said, shocked at the suggestion.

"Why not?" Lorian asked.

"Because it's forbidden. Because it's dangerous. Because we don't know enough. Because of a million reasons, all of them good ones."

"But no one would know," Lorian said. "You could do it, Dooku. You have a better Force connection than any Padawan. Everyone knows that. And with the help of the holobook, you'd succeed."

Dooku shook his head. He put the holobook back on the shelf.

"It would be amazing," Lorian said. "You could find out Sith secrets. If you really knew the dark side, you'd be a better Jedi Knight. Yoda says that we can't fight evil without understanding it."

"Yoda never said that."

"Well, it sounds like something he'd say," Lorian protested. "And it's true. Isn't that what Temple training is all about? All we do is study so we can be prepared. How can we prepare to meet evil if we don't understand it?"

That was the trouble with Lorian, Dooku thought. He had a way of putting things that made sense, even when he was asking you to break the rules.

He looked over at the holobook again. It *was* tempting. And Lorian had put his finger on Dooku's secret wish — to be the best Padawan ever. He wanted to impress his new Master. Could the Sith Holocron be the key to his wish?

"We'll only take a quick look," Lorian said. "Just think, Dooku. The Jedi are the most powerful group in the galaxy. We could be the best of the best."

"A true Jedi does not think in terms of power," Dooku said disapprovingly. "We are peacekeepers."

"Peacekeepers need power, just like everybody else," Lorian pointed out. "If they don't have it, who will listen?"

Lorian was right, even though he wasn't expressing himself in what would be considered a true Jedi way. The Jedi *did* have power. Jedi did not use that word, but it fit. Lorian knew that, and he wasn't afraid to say it. Jedi were renowned throughout the galaxy. They weren't feared, but they were respected. They were asked by governments, by Senators, for their help. If that wasn't power, what was?

The best of the best. Wasn't that what he wanted?

"Thame is a great Knight," Lorian continued. "I'd think you'd want to be worthy of him. If I had a Master, I'd prepare as much as I could before we left the Temple. I wouldn't want to disappoint him."

"I won't disappoint him if I do my best," Dooku said. "That is all I can do."

Lorian threw himself back on Thame's sleep couch with a groan. "Now *you* sound like Yoda."

"Don't sit there!" Dooku hissed, but Lorian ignored him.

Lorian stared at the ceiling. "No one has chosen me."

Dooku held his breath. Here it was, the big thing between them. He had been chosen by a Jedi Knight, and Lorian had not. Dooku had been one of the first to be chosen. Every day afterward, the two boys had waited for a Jedi Knight to choose Lorian. They knew that many had watched him, and some had considered him seriously. Yet each time, the Knight had chosen someone else. Neither Dooku nor Lorian knew why. Dooku had always been ahead of Lorian in battle skills and Force connection, but Lorian was just as brilliant in his studies and commitment. It was unthinkable that Lorian would not be chosen eventually.

"It will happen," Dooku said. "Patience exists to be tested."

Lorian flipped over on his side and gave Dooku a flat stare. "Right."

Dooku wished he could take back his words. They were so . . . correct. They were something a Jedi Master might say, not a best friend. But the truth was that he didn't know what to say. The period of waiting was hard, but everything would turn out all right.

Lorian coiled his body into a ball and then shot off the bed. "Okay, make a decision. Do we access the Sith Holocron or not?"

Dooku reached over to straighten the wrinkles Lorian had made on his new Master's bed. Thame was everything he'd hoped to get as a Master. He couldn't jeopardize that. Not even for his best friend.

"Not," he said. "We'd get in serious trouble if we got caught."

"You never worried about getting caught before," Lorian said.

That's because I never had so much to lose. But Dooku couldn't say that. If he did, it would only point out that Lorian didn't have a Master.

Dooku felt Lorian's eyes on his back as he bent to smooth the coverlet at the end of Thame's sleep couch.

"If you could do it without the risk of getting caught, you would do it," Lorian said. "So the fact that it's wrong isn't really the reason you won't. Maybe you're not the true Jedi you think you are."

He sauntered out the door. "Just wanted you to know that I noticed."

Now that Dooku was through with his official Temple training, he was allowed to structure his days himself. Although he was expected to continue to study and devote himself to battle training and physical discipline, it was also expected that he would allot the time for activities he enjoyed. In the brief period between a Padawan's last official classes and becoming an apprentice, the Jedi Masters indulged their students and gave them freedom to roam.

Dooku woke early. His conversation with Lorian the day before still troubled him. He decided to head to the Room of the Thousand Fountains to stroll among the greenery and let the music of the water calm his mind. It felt luxurious to be able to decide how to spend his time. He knew such days would be over soon, and he intended to enjoy every second of them. He wouldn't allow a small disagreement with his friend to ruin them, either.

He stepped out into the hallway and immediately noticed a change. Dooku sometimes wasn't sure whether the Force or his intuition was working — he wasn't that experienced yet. But he knew that the atmosphere in the

Temple had changed. There was a humming current underneath the calm, an agitation he could pick up easily.

Ahead of him, a few students stood in a cluster. Dooku approached them. He recognized Hran Beling, a fellow student his age. Hran was a Vicon, a small species only one meter tall.

He didn't have to ask the students what they were discussing. Hran looked up at him, his long nose twitching. "Have you heard the news? The Sith Holocron has been stolen!"

Dooku was naturally pale, but he felt his blood drain from his face, and he was sure he looked as white as a medic's gown. "What? How?"

"No one knows how," Hran said. "There could be an intruder at the Temple."

One of the younger students lowered his voice to a whisper. "What if it's a Sith?"

Hran's eyes twinkled. "Yes, what if it is?" he asked solemnly. "He could be walking the halls. He could be anywhere. What if he's behind you right now?" Hran gasped and pointed behind the young student, who jumped in alarm, his Padawan braid flying.

The others burst into nervous laughter. Dooku didn't join them. His heart thumping, he turned away.

There had been no intruder. He was sure of it.

Dooku hurried to Lorian's quarters. The privacy light was on over Lorian's door, but he accessed it anyway. The door was locked.

Dooku pressed his mouth against the seam of the door. "Let me in, Lorian."

There was no answer.

"Let me in or I'll go straight to the Jedi Council room," Dooku threatened.

He heard the smooth click as the lock disengaged, and the door slid open. The room was dark, the shade drawn against the rising sun. He stepped inside and the door hissed shut behind him. All was dark except for the hologram of *Caravan,* a model star cruiser Lorian had designed. It traveled the room in an endless loop.

Lorian sat in a corner, as if he were trying to press himself against the wall hard enough to melt inside it. His hands dangled between his knees, and Dooku saw that they were shaking.

"You took it."

"I didn't mean to," Lorian said. "I just wanted to look at it."

"Where is it?"

Lorian pointed to the far corner with his chin. "Do you feel it?" he whispered. "I feel so sick. . . ."

"Why did you take it?" Dooku asked sharply, his gaunt features making him look older than his years. Sweat broke out on his forehead. He could feel the dark power of the Holocron. He didn't want to look at it. Just knowing it was behind him in a dark corner was enough to make him feel shaky.

"I was in the archives. I had it in my hands. Someone

was coming. I put it underneath my cloak. Then I ran." Lorian shuddered. "I was going to take it back, but I can't . . . I can't touch it again, Dooku. I didn't expect it to be like this."

"How did you expect it to be?" Dooku asked angrily. "A pleasant walk in the woods?"

"I have to bring it back," Lorian said. "I need your help."

Dooku looked at him in disbelief. "I told you I didn't want anything to do with this."

"But you have to help me!" Lorian cried. "You're my best friend!"

"You got yourself into this," Dooku said. "Just stick it under your cloak again and bring it back."

"I can't do it alone, Dooku," Lorian said.

Dooku's gaze rested on Lorian's shaking hands. He didn't doubt that Lorian wouldn't be able to do it.

"Please, Dooku," Lorian begged.

Dooku didn't get a chance to answer. The door suddenly hissed open. Oppo Rancisis, Jedi Master and revered member of the Jedi Council, stood in the doorway.

"Are you ill, Lorian?" he asked kindly. "Some of the Masters noticed that you . . ." His voice trailed off. Dooku felt the atmosphere in the room change, as though gravity had increased. He felt it pressing against him.

Oppo Rancisis stared at them. "I sense a tremor in the Force," he said.

They could not speak.

His keen gaze swept the room. Suddenly he turned

and strode to the corner and picked up the Holocron. He placed it carefully in the deep pocket of his robe.

Then he turned and regarded the two boys.

Lorian pressed himself back against the wall and pushed himself to a standing position.

"It was Dooku's idea," he said.

CHAPTER No. 3

Dooku was too shocked to say a word.

"The Council will want to see you both," Oppo Rancisis said sternly.

"But I didn't —" Dooku began.

Oppo Rancisis held up a hand. "Whatever you have to say will be said before the Council. The truth will be spoken there." He turned and walked out.

"Dooku, listen —" Lorian started.

Rage filled Dooku. He couldn't even meet his friend's gaze.

He ran blindly down the hall. He didn't know where he was going. He had so many sanctuaries in the Temple — a favorite bench, a spot by a window, a rock by the lake — but he could not imagine any of those places offering him sanctuary now. His heart was so full of black anger and bitterness that he felt he was choking.

His best friend had betrayed him. Throughout the years at the Temple, he could always depend on Lorian. They had shared jokes and secrets. They had competed and helped each other. They had quarreled and made up.

The fact that this person could betray him shocked him so deeply he felt sick.

He didn't know how he passed the day. Somehow the news got out that the two had been caught. Students sent him sidelong looks and hurried by him. Jedi Knights who did not know him studied him as they passed in the hall. Dooku longed to go to Yoda and explain everything, but he knew that Yoda would only repeat what Oppo Rancisis had said. He had to suffer through the days until the Jedi Council found the time to speak to them.

Dooku did not have the appetite or the nerve to face the others in the dining hall for the evening meal. He stayed in his room. When at last the hallways glowed with the cool blue light that meant the Temple was settling down to sleep, he felt relief. At least for the next hours he wouldn't be under scrutiny.

He couldn't wait to be called before the Council. He couldn't wait to tell the truth. He knew the Masters would believe him and not Lorian. A Jedi Master was adept at discerning truth. Lorian would not get away with his lie, and Dooku would have justice.

He turned out the light and lay on his sleep couch, his heart burning. He imagined how clearly he would speak. He would tell the truth — all of it. He would tell them how Lorian tried to tempt him. He would tell them how he refused him, and how Lorian had pressed him. It was with great satisfaction that Dooku imagined Lorian's punishment. A reprimand would surely not go far enough. Lorian could even get expelled from the Jedi Order.

His door hissed open. He hadn't locked it. Dooku never locked his door. He'd never needed to, until now.

Lorian slipped into the dark room. Dooku said nothing, hoping his contempt would fill the space better than words.

Lorian sat on the floor, a few meters away from the sleep couch.

"I had a reason for saying what I did," he said.

"I'm not interested in your reasons."

"You don't understand anything," Lorian burst out. "Everything comes so easily to you. You never think about other people, about how they suffer. You just kept telling me I shouldn't worry about getting chosen. Why shouldn't I worry? Time is running out! It's so easy for you to say. You were picked right away."

"So you're blaming me for that?" Dooku hissed. "Is that why you lied to Oppo Rancisis?"

"No," Lorian said. "And I don't blame you for anything except not trying to understand how I feel. We're supposed to be best friends, and you never, ever really tried. All you think about is your own pleasure in your success."

"Get out of my room," Dooku said.

Instead, Lorian stretched out on the floor. His voice lowered. "Can't you understand, Dooku? I'm in trouble. I need your help. I know I was wrong. I shouldn't have taken the Holocron. But I was desperate. I thought if only I had an edge, if only I could know something that no one else knows. . . . Can't you understand why I would want that?"

"No," Dooku said. But he did.

"Now if the Council finds out I did it, I could be kicked out of the Jedi."

"You're exaggerating, as usual," Dooku said scathingly. But hadn't he been thinking the same thing?

"Everything is at stake for me," Lorian said. "But you've already been chosen by the great Thame Cerulian. Not only that, Master Yoda has taken a personal interest in you. The Council has watched you, too. They know you have an extraordinary Force connection. They'll forgive you. Especially since your Master is interested in the Sith. You could say you just wanted to do some research."

Lorian's voice floated up in the darkness, ragged with desperation. "I panicked when Oppo Rancisis came in. I saw my future, and it scared me. I could get kicked out, and where would I go, what would I do?"

"You should have thought of that before you stole the Sith Holocron."

"I know I shouldn't ask such a big thing, but who else can I ask but my best friend? Because no matter what, you're still my best friend." Lorian paused. For a moment, all Dooku could hear was their breathing. "Will you cover for me?"

Dooku wanted to burst out with a savage "No!" But he couldn't. He didn't know if Lorian could get kicked out of the order — he didn't think so. But it served Lorian right to have to worry about it.

Punishment would be severe for him, especially since he'd tried to lie and cover up. But Lorian was right — Dooku was a favorite of the Jedi Masters. He knew how he could tell the story so that he would just get a lecture, most likely. He would let them think it was a hunger for knowledge, a desire to impress his new Master. They would believe that.

Dooku didn't know what to say. He wasn't prepared to lie, but he couldn't say no to his friend. So he said nothing, and, after a long while, the two friends fell asleep.

CHAPTER No. 4

Dooku woke before dawn. Lying in the dark, he listened to the silence and knew that Lorian had left sometime during the night. He lay on his back, feeling the weight of the air on his body as though his friend was sitting on his chest.

Reluctant to rise, he stared at the walls, watching the darkness slowly silver into gray, until he could see the outlines of his furniture. The light on his bedside table began to glow softly and increase in intensity, his signal to wake up. Then a holographic calendar appeared and glowed in the air overhead. Usually the day calendar had been filled with appointments and classes. Lately he had liked looking at its blankness. Soon he would fill it up with missions.

He stared at it, thinking of his future. It was secure. Was Lorian right? Had he been smug about that and failed to appreciate his friend's distress?

He stared at the calendar for long minutes, thinking of this, before it registered on his brain that the entire day had been blocked out. Dooku sat up. The urban search exercise! It was today! Not only that, he saw that he and Lorian had been summoned before the Jedi Council following the search.

The exercise was designed more for competitive fun than for serious training. The older students, the ones who had either been chosen as apprentices or who had finished their formal Temple training, were invited to sign up. They were divided into two teams, and had to track one another through a segment of Coruscant near the Temple. They had to use stealth, cunning, and surveillance techniques. Dooku and Lorian had signed up the week before.

Dooku swung his legs over the bed. Would he and Lorian still be allowed to participate?

He dressed hurriedly and grabbed his training lightsaber. He walked out into the hallway and saw Yoda ahead. Yoda nodded a greeting.

"Heading to the tracking exercise, are you?" Yoda asked.

"I—I don't know if I am permitted . . ." Dooku stammered.

Yoda cocked his head at him. "A commitment you made. A Padawan you are. And thus the answer you find is . . ."

"I'm going," Dooku said. He hurried off. He had just enough time to grab some fruit for the morning meal before the students assembled outside on the landing platform. He wondered if Lorian would have the nerve to show up.

Lorian stood at the edge of the small crowd on the exterior platform. He was clearly uncomfortable and avoided standing too near or too far away. He wore his hood low so that it shaded his eyes. Dooku stood at the edge of the group, opposite from Lorian. No one paid attention to them. Whatever the gossip had been, it had died down, and the students now only thought of the contest ahead.

The cool morning air flushed their cheeks and the wind whipped their robes around them as they chattered in excited voices. Dooku felt the combined Force from the group, energetic, unfocused, but strong.

For a moment he stood outside himself. It was something that happened to him from time to time. Suddenly he would feel removed, as though he floated above his classmates.

How young we all are, he thought, amused. *Someday I will look back on this and wish for such simple things as a learning exercise on a cool morning.*

It made him feel better for a moment. Someday his problem with Lorian wouldn't matter. It would be a blip, a moment of static, something lost in a sea of missions in a remarkable career.

Then Yoda and Oppo Rancisis emerged from the interior of the Temple. His gaze rested on Dooku only briefly, but it brought Dooku back to reality with a bump. His mood suddenly soured as he thought of the Jedi Council he would have to face.

The students quieted as Yoda approached. He stood in the middle of the group, nodding greetings at the familiar faces. He'd known them all since they were babies and had trained them all when they were younglings.

"In an exercise know you do that every year the oldest students participate," he said. "Urban tracking, this year's will be. That this is a test remember you must. Yet graded you will not be. Take it seriously but lightly you must. Attempt to win you will; if you lose, enjoy it you may."

The students smiled at Yoda's contradictions and fiddled with their training lightsabers. Everyone was anxious to begin.

"And now, the rules," Oppo said. "You will be divided into two teams of ten. In a moment, your team color will flash on your datapad. Each team will have a different starting point. The goal of each team is to successfully bring a muja fruit from one of the fruitsellers in the All Planets Market back to the Temple by sunset. Team members can be eliminated only by one light touch with a lightsaber."

The students smiled. They knew that no matter how easy it sounded, the actual exercise would turn out to be much harder.

"You must keep to the segment mapped out on your datapad. To cross the line is to be disqualified. Do you understand this?"

The students nodded, trying to conceal their anticipation. They all knew the rules.

Yoda nodded, letting them know that their attempts to hide their impatience hadn't fooled him a bit. "Perhaps wait you should until the sun is higher. . . ." he began, his eyes twinkling.

"No, please, Master Yoda!" the students chorused the words together.

"Ah, then teams you will become. Look on your data-pads, you must."

The students reached for the palm-sized datapads on their utility belts. Dooku's screen glowed blue.

"Blue and gold, the team colors are," Yoda said. "And the captains are these: Dooku for blue, Lorian for gold. Waiting, the Jedi Masters are, to take you to your starting points."

Startled, Dooku looked first at Yoda, then at Lorian, whose blank face showed how deeply surprised he was. Why had they been chosen as captains? Maybe yesterday morning they would have been chosen. Yesterday morning, when they were not suspected of stealing a Sith Holocron. Yesterday morning, when they were still Padawans in good standing.

Dooku gripped his datapad, still reeling by Yoda's words. He had not yet completely figured out Jedi logic, that was certain.

"Hey, Dooku, wake up!" Hran Beling grinned at him as he tugged on the sleeve of his tunic. "Is it a little early for you?"

"Jedi Master Reesa Doliq is waiting," Galinda Norsh said briskly. "Let's get started."

Dooku noticed that the Gold Team members were

all scrambling to board a transport. He hurried behind the other Blue Team members to get aboard their own transport. Reesa Doliq smiled at the students as they crammed in.

"Room for everyone," she said. "Don't worry, I'll have you at the starting point in no time. In the meantime, you can start on your strategy."

The two transports lifted off. Dooku found that every Blue Team member was staring at him, waiting for him to begin. He was the leader, after all.

He cleared his throat and looked down at his datapad. The map of the area they would be operating in flashed onscreen. Dooku was familiar with much of it. It consisted of the Senate buildings, several grand boulevards that he knew quite well, and the All Planets Market, which was held in a large plaza near the Senate complex. As a promising student of diplomacy, he had signed up for special tutorials in Senate procedure, so he'd had plenty of opportunities to explore the Senate grounds.

Quickly Dooku scanned the map, trying to locate streets and alleys and space lanes. Everyone had to be coordinated and a strategy must be devised. They should spread out and each student should get a muja fruit. That would increase the odds of their win.

But why? Dooku thought suddenly. It was just what Lorian would expect him to do, so why should he do it?

"Our starting coordinate is Nova level," Galinda said. "That's good. There are many alleys there to hide in. And

the gravsleds and truck transports will be unloading sup-
plies for the market. We can use them for cover." She
looked over Dooku's shoulder at the map.

Hran Beling nodded. "We can pick the fastest among
us to pick up the fruit."

"They'll probably be staking out the fruit stands,"
Galinda said. "We have to get there first."

"Maybe not," Dooku muttered, his head bent over the
map.

"Do you have a better idea?" Hran asked.

Dooku didn't answer. He was thinking. What would
Lorian expect him to do?

*He would expect me to race to get a muja fruit first. He
would expect me to send three Padawans to retrieve the
fruit, and guard them with the rest. If they all didn't make
it, I'd send back two.*

He looked at the map again.

"Do you have a plan or, what?" Galinda asked impatiently.

Dooku looked up at last. "Yes," he said. "We're not going after the muja fruit at all."

They looked at him skeptically. Dooku only smiled. He
would bend them to his will. He would make them see his
strategy. Because he knew one thing on this day: He had
to win.

CHAPTER No. **5**

"Why expose ourselves to get the fruit at the start?" Dooku asked them. "Why not let the Gold Team try for the fruit, and pick them off one by one? We might lose a few team members, but not as many as they will. When you are intent on getting something, you take more chances. Then, when no Gold Team members are left, we can simply stroll to the market, pick a fruit, and head back to the Temple. Simple."

"Sure, if we're able to pick them all off," Galinda said. "What if one of them gets through and makes it back to the Temple?"

"That is not an acceptable outcome," Dooku said. His coolness made the others exchange glances. Dooku had learned early that in order to inspire confidence he should not admit doubt.

Galinda was still skeptical. "But where can we set up surveillance? There's not much cover in the market. We need good sight lines."

"I have a plan for that, too," Dooku said.

Dooku stood as the transport landed. He noticed that

Master Doliq was watching him curiously. He tucked his datapad into his belt. "Follow me," he told the others.

He jumped off the ramp and led the way through the twisting streets to the Senate complex. He walked so purposefully that no one asked him where they were going.

When he arrived at the complex he led the others onto a turbolift and descended to the lower sub-offices. He had a foolproof strategy. It just depended on his powers of persuasion and how much a friend of his was willing to bend the rules. He was learning that sometimes it was better to come at things sideways, especially when his opponent assumed he would come at them head-on. Persuasion and deception could work better than battles.

Dooku turned to the others as he reached a door. "Wait here. I'll just be a minute."

He accessed the door and walked in. A tall, spindly creature with waving antennae and bright yellow eyes sat at a datascreen. He looked up and saw Dooku, then pretended to tremble.

"Dooku! Oh, no! Have you come to show me up again?"

"Not at all, Eero." Dooku smiled. His first meeting with the young Senatorial aide Eero Iridian had cemented their friendship, but not in the usual way. Dooku had been attending a seminar on the political history of the Correllian system. Eero had read a paper he'd written on the subject, and Dooku had raised a hand to correct a number of points he felt were inaccurate. Eero had bristled at the newcomer, but a quick search of the archives had revealed that Dooku had been right.

Eero had been hoping to impress both his father, a Senator, and his boss. Instead, he'd been publicly embarrassed. Yet after the seminar he'd come up to Dooku and asked if the student would be interested in joining his study group. He'd been annoyed at Dooku, but he wanted to learn from him, too. Dooku had joined the group for a time, and he and Eero had become friends. Eero's father was powerful and Eero longed to follow in his footsteps. Dooku admired how hard he studied and the fact that he took the job of a Senatorial aide so seriously.

Of course that was not why he had come to see him today.

"I need a favor," Dooku said.

"Anything I have is yours," Eero declared.

"I need your code card to the C level transport hallway," Dooku said.

"Except that," Eero said.

Dooku said nothing. He just waited.

Eero fiddled with a flexible antennae. "Okay, why?"

"A Padawan exercise," Dooku said. "I need the element of surprise, and that passage overlooks the All Planets Market. There's also an exit with a turbolift straight down to market level. We can use it as a base."

"But it's restricted to Senate personnel."

"That's why I need your access card," Dooku said patiently. Eero's fault as a scholar, he recalled, was that he had trouble putting different facts together to reach a conclusion. He noted the reluctance on Eero's face. Maybe he should offer a favor as an exchange. This was the Senate, after all.

"I'll help you with that Tolfranian brief that's giving you so much trouble," Dooku offered.

Eero looked torn. "I could use the help. But I could get in trouble with Senate security if I give you the code card. It could go on my record. On the other hand, this brief is really important to my boss. . . ." Eero began to fiddle furiously with both antennae now, twirling them around his fingers until they sprang loose in coils. "Okay," he finally said in a rush of breath. He tossed the code card to Dooku.

"I'll have it back to you by this evening," Dooku said, hurrying out.

Now I have you, Lorian. You won't beat me.

The plan worked perfectly . . . for a while. Dooku and the team had a perfect view of the muja fruitseller from a window in a storage area. They could clearly see the bustling market and the fact that Lorian and the Gold Team members had set up several stakeout areas. They were waiting for Dooku to strike. Dooku knew that Lorian believed the Blue Team would make an aggressive first move. It was usually how Dooku began a lightsaber battle. But a trademark move could betray you. It was better to mix up tactics. Lorian had no idea that he, too, had a trademark move. When he began to lose a battle, he made a deliberately wide pass to the left, then spun around to his opponent's rear. This gave him precious seconds to catch his breath and compose his mind.

Dooku sent out his group in pairs. They communicated by comlink. From their perch above they were able to track the evasive procedures the other team employed. It was easy to direct their team members below. With a slight touch of the lightsaber, one after another, Gold Team members went down. Each hit was recorded on everyone's datapad.

They were winning. Lorian's team had managed to hit only one Blue Team member, and they'd taken out five of his.

Then Lorian must have figured out what they were doing.

Suddenly Dooku saw two Gold team members running toward the turbolift. Unable to access it, they began to use their cable launchers to scale the glass tube. They would find a way in. That left three Gold members. If Dooku were Lorian, he would try to ambush them at an exit.

Or Lorian would go for the muja fruit while he was running from him.

No, Dooku thought. *Lorian knows the Senate well. He will think he can catch me here.*

Just in case, Dooku barked into his comlink at his two team members in the market. "Guard that fruitseller. We have to abandon the surveillance post." He turned to the remaining six members of his team. "Let's get out of here."

The team members raced out of the storage unit. There was only one other way down — through the turbolift that connected to the Senate main halls. Dooku thought rapidly as the turbolift sank downward. Lorian had also attended seminars in the Senate. Lorian knew the building even better than Dooku. Lorian loved poking around in places he shouldn't. If he didn't know before that this turbolift led to only two exits, he had no doubt made it his business to know. It would have been easy to access a Senate map and find out.

Dooku reached out and pressed the button to stop the turbolift. "We're not getting out," he told the others. "We're going up."

He leaped up and balanced on the handrail. He accessed the escape hatch at the top and climbed up. Above his head was a door leading to a Senate level. A training lightsaber did not have the power of a true lightsaber, but it could most likely get through the metal door over his head.

He worked his lightsaber along the seam of the door. "Galinda, Hran, I need some help," he called down as he worked.

The two Padawans squirmed up through the opening. They got out their lightsabers to help him. Within minutes they had peeled back the metal just enough for them to squeeze through.

They crawled through the opening. Dooku saw an orientation kiosk and hurriedly accessed the Senate map. He found the fastest route to an exit.

"We have about three to five minutes before Lorian figures out that we're not coming out of that turbolift and we're no longer in hallway C," Dooku said. "That's enough time to buy some muja fruit, I think."

Stained and dirty now from the turbolift tunnel, the rest of the team grinned as they tucked their lightsabers into their utility belts. Winning was so close now they could taste it.

They ran down the hallway toward the exit. They burst into the open air and ran in the direction of the market. The sun was high overhead now, but clouds were beginning to gather. Shade and shadow dappled them as they dodged shoppers and carts and made their way toward the fruitsellers.

Suddenly Dooku wished they had formed a plan before they'd charged into the market. They were all running full-tilt, all of them hoping to be the first to buy a muja fruit and got it back safely to the Temple. He had lost his focus because the end was so near.

His datascreen flashed. His other two Blue Team members, the ones in the market, had been hit. Lorian hadn't set up an ambush in the Senate after all.

"They're in the market!" Dooku yelled. "Split up!"

A blur of red, then green came to Dooku out of the corner of his eye. He stopped so quickly he almost fell backward into a display of children's toys. Members of the Gold Team were charging at his team, their lightsabers held discreetly at their sides, but ready to strike. He saw Hran get tapped and he turned away, a disgusted look on his face. Galinda held a muja fruit in her hands as Lorian suddenly appeared from behind an awning. His lightsaber whirled gracefully and came down with the slightest touch on the back of her shoulder. Galinda winced. Lorian smiled, plucked the muja out of her hand, and tucked it into his tunic.

Now each team had five members left. It was a tie. Dooku had lost his lead.

Lorian threw a glance at Dooku through the crowd. Dooku saw a playful challenge in his friend's gaze. Fury coursed through him. He didn't feel playful.

This isn't a game, he thought. *Not for me.*

Dooku leaped over the display of toys. He snaked around a couple with a baby in a repulsorlift carrier. He dived under a table, rolled, and came up behind a Gold Team member. He struck him lightly between the shoulder blades. He didn't stay to notice his reaction, but moved on, striking another team member from behind, then moving in to engage in battle with another. He dodged the whirling lightsaber and kicked at a jar of syrup on display. It smashed on the floor, the Jedi student slipped, and Dooku claimed another hit. He did not pause but ran full-tilt toward another Gold Team member who was racing toward the fruitseller. Dooku accessed the

Force and leaped. Usually his control wasn't the best for this maneuver — he still had much to learn — but he surprised himself with perfect execution. He landed in front of the student and simply tapped his shoulder.

Breathing hard, Dooku glanced at his datapad. Lorian's strike had been successful. Every one of his team members had been hit. But he had managed to take out the rest of Lorian's team. That made them even. Except for the fact that Lorian had a muja fruit.

No time to get the fruit. If he got Lorian, he'd get the muja. He'd make it to the Temple and deposit it politely right into the hands of Master Yoda.

The Padawans had all trudged off, some in pairs or groups, to make their way back to the Temple. They were not allowed to help their captains. Lorian had disappeared into the crowd.

Think, Dooku. Don't act until you think. Dooku called on the Force to help him. At first he saw only beings and goods in the market. He concentrated, waiting until his brain registered the familiar. A certain tilt of the head. A step. An angle of the chin. Some movement so tiny that his senses would pick it up in a sea of information that he couldn't process. But the Force could.

The Force surged. Everything fell away, and he saw Lorian. Cleverly he had reversed his cloak so that the darker underside was out. Dooku set off after him. He would not make the same mistake again. He would wait for his moment.

He stayed well behind Lorian. He didn't think Lorian knew he was on his trail. Lorian headed out of the market and turned down an alley that Dooku wasn't familiar with. Leave it to Lorian to find all the back ways in Coruscant. Dooku faded back, careful to stay out of sight. It was afternoon now, and the sun had dropped behind heavy cloud cover. It was almost as dark as evening, and the glowlights were on their lowest setting.

The alley twisted back behind the market and made a sharp left turn, now snaking along the back entrances of a variety of shops and restaurants. The odor of garbage was strong. Dooku put his cloak over his nose. He had a fastidious nature. He liked cleanliness and order.

To Dooku's surprise, the Temple suddenly loomed ahead. They were much closer than he'd thought. His heartbeat raced. Lorian was in sight of winning! He couldn't let that happen. He had to strike now.

Gathering the Force, Dooku leaped. He landed on a soft heap of garbage, which gave him plenty of spring. *Garbage is good for something, after all,* he thought as the momentum sent him skyward. He flew over Lorian's head and landed in front of him, lightsaber activated. He did not wait to absorb the shock of his landing but used the bounce for his charge.

Lorian had less than a second to adjust, but his reflexes were excellent, a source of envy among the other students. He leaped backward, reaching for his lightsaber and tilting his move so that Dooku's first strike whistled through the air.

"So you found me," he said. He seemed delighted, not dismayed. Their friendship had been built on competition. It had always been fun. But Lorian's reaction only enraged Dooku. He resented Lorian's ease, his assumption that they would always be friends, no matter what. That's what made Lorian push the boundary of their friendship. He pushed too hard. Then he expected Dooku to take it.

There was a flash of surprise on Lorian's face when he noted the coldness in Dooku's gaze. He stumbled backward as Dooku came at him furiously, his lightsaber a blur of color and motion.

Lorian recovered almost instantly. He counterattacked in a series of aggressive moves while Dooku was forced on the defensive.

The two friends knew each other's moves so well by now. Again and again Dooku tried to surprise Lorian, but he was checked every time. Frustration built in him, clouding his mind. He knew he had to find his calm center in order to win, but he couldn't. He had lost his battle mind.

They fought down the length of the alley, using the garbage bins as cover and occasionally as weapons, pushing the bins toward each other in order to gain a precious moment or two to take a breath.

Time stopped. Dooku was lost in the battle, lost in his own sweat and his own need to win. They were both tired now. Lorian's face was bright red with effort, and his hair was wet. Every so often they both had to stop, exhausted, and lean over to catch their breaths. Then one of them would recover more quickly and launch himself at the other. Their grunts and cries echoed down the alleyway.

Time may have stopped, but the sun still moved. Long shadows snaked down the alley floor. It was past time for them to return to the Temple. By the rules, they had both already lost.

"Come on, Dooku," Lorian said. "It's over."

Dooku took several ragged breaths. Spots had formed in front of his eyes, a sign that he was seriously exhausted. He felt dizzy. He reached for the Force. It was elusive. Instead of flowing through him, he could barely feel it trickle. But it was enough to send a small spurt of strength through his limbs.

"Not yet," he said, attacking Lorian.

Lorian was at the end of the alley now. He had only a few steps before his back would be against the wall. Dooku knew he could finish him there.

But Lorian suddenly turned, leaving his back exposed for a split second, and ran at the wall. He used a basic Padawan exercise, but Dooku was surprised he still had the strength. He ran up the wall, then flipped over Dooku's head. As soon as he landed, he leaped again, this time on a pile of garbage. From there he gained the roof overhead.

Dooku found the strength he was looking for. He followed Lorian's path, launching onto the garbage and then to the roof so quickly and gracefully it seemed one long, continuous movement.

The breeze had sharpened and quickened, and it gave them fresh energy. Dooku flew toward Lorian, putting extra strength into his moves, his footwork sure despite the uneven material of the roof.

"You hate me, don't you?" Lorian grunted, parrying a thrust. "Just because I finally asked something of you."

"Something it wasn't fair of you to ask."

"That is what friendship is."

"Not my definition."

"Yes, your definition is that someone gives and you take. Someone admires you and you accept that admiration." Lorian was breathing hard now. "Someone you can use."

"You have always resented me," Dooku said. "Now I know how much."

He drove forward. Lorian's words filled with him anger. He knew he was only supposed to touch Lorian to win, but that inability to reach him, to even graze his skin, had built up the frustration to a boiling point. His body felt hot.

Lorian made a half-turn to the left and swung out in a wide arc.

I have him now. He knows he's losing. It was Lorian's trademark move.

Dooku already knew Lorian would spring to his rear. If

Lorian hadn't been so tired, he wouldn't have tried it. Instead of moving to the left, Dooku moved back two steps. When Lorian came at him, he was ready. He brought his lightsaber down on Lorian's shoulder, right where his tunic had torn along the seam.

Lorian cried out and stumbled back. He looked at Dooku with disbelief. It had been a true blow, designed to hurt.

"You gravel maggot," he said. He sprang at Dooku.

Now they fought without regard for rules of engagement. They fought hard, using every trick. They used their feet and fists as well as their lightsabers. They kicked at each other and struck out blindly as they moved by. Dooku had never fought like this. In a part of his mind he knew that this style of fighting brought him nothing, that it was sloppy and unfocused and would turn them both into losers, but he couldn't stop.

"Enough."

The word was spoken quietly but it cut through the sound of their battle. They stopped. Yoda had appeared on the roof. They hadn't noticed him. They hadn't noticed that their battle had brought them within sight of the Temple windows, either.

Yoda walked over to Lorian. Dooku saw now that the lightsaber blow had left a deep bruise on Lorian's bare arm. It looked terrible, the center a deep red with a blue-black bruise surrounding it. Lorian had a cut on his cheek and one hand was bleeding.

"To the med clinic go you must, Lorian," Yoda said. "Dooku, to your quarters. Send for you both we will."

Lorian's gaze rested on the ground. He lifted his head. His eyes met Dooku's. In that moment everything formed into a hard knot of certainty in Dooku's heart. They were enemies now.

CHAPTER No. 6

Dooku stood before the Jedi Council. He did not know if Lorian had come before him or would be appearing after. He only knew one thing: It was time to tell the truth. He described how Lorian had wanted them to take the Sith Holocron, and later, how Lorian had asked him to lie for him.

"And were you prepared to lie for him?" Oppo Rancisis asked.

Dooku took a moment before answering. He wanted to lie and say that he had never considered Lorian's request, yet he knew the Jedi Masters could see through him like water. He wasn't as powerful as they were, not yet.

"I was not prepared to lie, no," Dooku said. "I thought about it. Lorian was my friend."

"No longer your friend, is he?" Yoda asked.

This he could answer without getting mired in doubt and hesitation. The truth was clear. "No. He is no longer my friend."

"Clear to us is this as well," Yoda said. "A training lightsaber is not meant to wound, yet wound Lorian you did."

"I did not mean to," Dooku said. "I was angry and my control was not the best. My best friend had betrayed me."

"Lost control you did," Yoda said. "And too old for excuses you are."

Dooku nodded and looked down. He had expected this rebuke, but he had not expected it to sting so badly. He had never disappointed Yoda before.

"Tension between you there was, controlled the anger should have been," Yoda went on. "Used the exercise for feelings you should have let go in other ways you did. Meditation. Discussion."

"Physical exercise," Tor Difusal broke in. "A conference with a Jedi Master. You know the outlets available to you. Yet you chose not to use them."

Dooku saw that he had been tricked. He had no doubt now that he and Lorian had been made team captains deliberately. The Jedi Council had wanted to pit them against each other to see how deep the tensions ran.

"Tricked you were not," Yoda said, as if he'd read Dooku's thoughts. "Given an opportunity you were. Not alone are you, Dooku. To ask for help is no shame."

"I know that." He had been told it enough times.

"Know this you do, but practice it you must," Yoda said sharply. "Conquer your pride, you must. Your flaw, it is."

"I will, Master Yoda." Dooku almost sighed aloud. Would he never get away from lessons?

"Go you may," Yoda said.

"Your decision?"

"You will hear of it," Tor Difusal said.

There was nothing to do but bow and leave. Dooku

heard the door slip shut silently behind him. Only a few words had been spoken, but he felt as though he had emerged from a battle.

The Jedi Council did not make them wait long. Dooku received a reprimand for excessive aggression during the exercise. Lorian was expelled from the Jedi Order, not for stealing the Sith Holocron, but for lying and implicating his friend.

Dooku felt relief course through him. He hadn't felt in danger of being expelled, but the affair could have had worse complications. Thame Cerulian could have dropped him as an apprentice. That had been his worst fear.

He took the turbolift up to the landing platform. It had always been one of his favorite places. He and Lorian had sneaked in here as younglings, hiding in a corner and naming all the starships. They'd imagined the day when they'd be the Jedi Knights striding through, hoisting themselves up into their cockpits and zooming off into the atmosphere.

He strolled down the aisle as the mechanic droids buzzed over the ships, doing routine maintenance. Now the time that he would be leaving was approaching. Thame was returning in three days. He could be off on a mission within a week.

He saw ahead that the exit door to the exterior platform was open. Someone must be leaving or arriving. He walked out. The clouds had gone and the night was crystal clear. The stars hung close and glittered so hard and bright it felt as though they could cut pieces in the sky.

He wasn't alone. Lorian stood on the platform, looking out over Coruscant.

"You've heard," he said.

"I'm sorry," Dooku said.

"Are you?" Lorian asked the question softly. "I hear no sorrow in your voice."

"I am sorry," Dooku said, "but you have to admit that you got yourself into this mess."

Lorian turned. His eyes glittered like the stars above, and Dooku realized there were tears in them. "A mess? Is that what you call it? How typical of you. Nothing touches you, Dooku. My life is *over*. I'm never going to be a Jedi! Can you imagine how that feels?"

"Why do you keep asking me to feel what you feel?" Dooku burst out. "I can't do that. I'm not you!"

"No, you're not me. But I know you better than anyone. I've seen more of what's inside you than anyone." Lorian took a step toward him. "I've seen your heart, and I know how empty it is. I've seen your anger, and I know how deep it is. I've seen your ambition, and I know how ruthless it is. And all of that will ultimately destroy you."

"You don't know what you're talking about," Dooku said. "You wanted me to lie to protect you. Do you think you're better than me?"

"No, that was never what it was about," Lorian said. "It was about friendship."

"That's exactly what it was about! You've always been jealous of me! That's why you wanted to destroy me. Instead," Dooku said, "you've destroyed yourself."

Lorian shook his head. He walked past Dooku, back toward the darkness of the hangar. "I know one thing," he said, his voice trailing behind him, but clear and even. "I will never be a Jedi, it's true. But neither will you. You will never never be a great Jedi Master."

Lorian and his words were swallowed up by the darkness. Dooku's cheeks burned despite the coolness of the air. Words crowded in his throat, threatening to break free. Then he decided he would let Lorian have the last word. Why not? He had the career. Lorian had nothing.

Lorian had been wrong. Dooku's heart hadn't been empty. He had loved his friend.

But he had changed. Lorian had betrayed him. He would never believe in friendship again. If his heart was now empty of love, so be it. The Jedi did not believe in attachments. He would fill his heart with nobility and passion and commitment. He *would* become a great Jedi Master.

Dooku looked up at a sky that glittered with stars and hummed with planets. So much to see, so much to do. So many beings to fight and to fight for. And yet he would take away from his time at the Temple one lesson, the most important one of all: In the midst of a galaxy crowded with life-forms, he was alone.

Dooku was blindfolded and playing with a seeker when he felt a presence enter the room. He knew it was Yoda. He could feel the way the Force gathered in the room. He continued to play with the seeker, swinging his lightsaber so the wind batted it gently, teasing it. He circled, listening and moving, knowing he could slice the seeker in two whenever he wanted.

Yoda had not spoken to him since Lorian had left the Temple. Dooku passed the time waiting for Thame to return, performing classic Jedi training exercises, wanting to impress the Council with his commitment.

"Of your ability, sure you are," Yoda said mildly. "Yet between sureness and pride, a small step it is."

Dooku stopped for a moment. He had wanted to impress Yoda, not provoke a rebuke. The seeker buzzed around his head like an angry insect.

"Fitting it is that blindfolded you are," Yoda continued. "Pride it is that blinds you. Your flaw, pride is. Great are your gifts, Dooku. Mindful of the talents you do not possess as well as the ones you do you must be."

Dooku heard only the slightest whisper of the fabric of

Yoda's robe as the Jedi Master retreated. The Force drained from the room.

Dooku was not used to criticism. He was the gifted one. He was the one the teachers always pointed to as an example. He hated to be corrected. Coolly, he struck out with his lightsaber and severed the seeker in two.

Thirteen Years Later

Dooku and Qui-Gon Jinn

Over the years, Dooku had thought of Yoda's words often. They were more a legacy than a lesson, for they were with him still.

He thought of them, but he did not accept them. He had not yet encountered a situation where his pride was his downfall. He did not think of it as pride, anyway. It was assurance. Assurance of his abilities merely grew with each mission, as it should. Yoda had mistaken sureness for pride, which is exactly what he had warned Dooku not to do.

And if it was pride for Dooku to think of himself as wiser than Yoda in this instance, Dooku wasn't concerned. Yoda was not always right. Dooku was not as great a Jedi as Yoda — not yet. But he would be one day. If he could not believe that, what was he working for?

Dooku had learned much from Thame Cerulian. Now he was a Master with an apprentice. Qui-Gon Jinn had been the most promising of the Padawans, and Dooku had maneuvered to get him the first time he saw him in lightsaber training, at ten years old. Dooku knew that a Master would be judged by the prowess of his Padawan, and he wanted the best of the best. When Yoda had given his approval of the match, Dooku had been satisfied. Another step had been taken toward his goal — to surpass Yoda as the greatest Jedi ever.

Luxury did not impress Dooku, but he did appreciate elegance. Senator Blix Annon had a beautiful starship, gleaming outside and all luxury within. In addition, the Senator had spared no expense in defensive systems. The starship's armor was triple-plated, with energy and particle shields, and front and rear laser cannons. It was a little large for Dooku's taste, but it was impressive.

He could tell that Qui-Gon was dazzled by the plush seating, the brushed durasteel facings on the instrument panels, and the silky, soft bedding in the quarters. Qui-Gon was only sixteen and what he'd seen of the galaxy so far had not shown him the luxurious side of life. Their missions lately had been on dreary planets or isolated outposts in the Outer Rim.

Dooku had been glad when they had been summoned back to Coruscant, although under normal circumstances he would consider this mission beneath him. He was simply an escort, a mission any Jedi could do. Lately there had been a series of kidnappings of Senators while they traveled between their homeworlds and Coruscant. The Senators and sometimes their families were held for enormous ransoms, which were always paid. No one knew the identity of the space pirate, and efforts to catch him had been unsuccessful. Dooku wasn't surprised. Senate security did well with protecting the Senators within the Senate building, but when it came to a galaxy-wide search, they were hopeless.

Blix Annon was an important Senator who had done many favors for the Jedi, and when he requested their presence, the Jedi Council had not only agreed, but had asked Dooku if he would take the assignment. A little weary of bad food and bleak surroundings, Dooku had considered a short flight on a luxurious cruiser not such a bad idea, with the additional benefit that it would give Qui-Gon an inside look at a Senator's entourage.

Senators never traveled alone. Blix Annon felt the need to travel with a speechwriter, a secretary, a chef, a hairdresser for the elaborate style he wore, and an aide whose sole function seemed to be to hover at his elbow, waiting to approve of whatever he said. That aide turned out to be Eero Iridian, Dooku's old friend.

When Dooku had arrived at the Senate landing pad, he had been as surprised to see his friend as Eero was to see him. They had done favors for each other over the years, but after Eero had lost the election for Senator of his homeworld for the second time, he had dropped out of public life. Dooku had lost track of him. Now he had turned up as an aide to one of the most important politicians in the Senate.

Dooku sat and stretched out his long legs. It had been

good to see Eero again, good to remember the boy he had been. They had talked about those years, about how mystifying the various rules of the Senate had been (admitting, with a laugh, that many were still mystifying). Then they'd talked about the dreams they'd had. Dooku had achieved his — he was a Jedi Knight, traveling throughout the galaxy. Despite his heritage, Eero had never achieved his dream of becoming a Senator. By the time his father retired, the old Senator had run through the family fortune. Eero had contacts but no wealth, and wealth was what won elections.

Now Eero dropped into the seat next to him with a sigh. "I've just been talking with your apprentice. Well, he didn't talk much, but I did. He's a good listener, that young man. I probably said more than I'd meant to about my Senate experiences."

Dooku nodded. He had noted this ability of Qui-Gon's. Beings told him things, and then were surprised that they had said so much. This could be good or bad, depending. Good if you were in the market for information. Bad if you were looking for peace and quiet on a journey and a scruffy space pilot was telling Qui-Gon his life story.

"He will be a great Jedi Knight," Dooku said. He had no doubt of that. Qui-Gon was quick to learn and very strong in the living Force. Dooku never had to tell him anything twice. If he could get rid of Qui-Gon's rather irritating tendency to befriend every scoundrel and vagabond they came across, the boy would be a perfect Padawan.

"I showed him the safe room," Eero said. "He was very impressed."

"It impressed me, too," Dooku said. The safe room was an additional security measure. In the event they were boarded, the Senator could retreat there. The door was blast-proof — the only way to break it down would be to use enough explosives to destroy the ship itself.

"I just hope we never have to use it," Eero said, his eyes scanning the expanse of space outside the window.

"I'm sure you will not, but we're prepared for anything," Dooku said.

Eero gave him a nervous look. "The ship is impregnable. That's what the security experts told us."

"No ship is impregnable," Dooku corrected. "That's why the Jedi are aboard."

He saw Qui-Gon hover in the doorway and waved him in.

"Do you need me, Master?" Qui-Gon asked respectfully.

Dooku gave his apprentice a small smile. "Yes. I need you to enjoy the trip. Mind the present moment, Padawan. We have a chance to rest and relax. We do not know when it will come again."

Qui-Gon nodded and seated himself a short distance away. He did not stretch out as Dooku was doing, but he did look a bit more relaxed as he glanced out the window. Dooku always admired his apprentice's manner. Even at sixteen, Qui-Gon had a quiet grace. Qui-Gon also had a quality of reserve that Dooku should also have admired. Yet somehow he found it frustrating not to know what his own apprentice was thinking most of the time.

"Allow me to make up a tray for us," Eero said, rising. "We have some excellent pastries. The Senator's chef —" Eero stopped abruptly as a sharp buzz came from the pilot's instruments. "What's that?"

"Nothing to be alarmed about," Dooku said, glancing over. "The pilot has the warning system activated. A ship is within our airspace, that's all." Despite his words, he kept an eye on the instruments, noting that Qui-Gon was doing so as well.

"A small cruiser," the pilot said aloud. "Everything seems normal . . . except . . ."

"Except?" Dooku leaned forward.

"There's no airspeed. The ship is dead in space."

Alarmed, Eero looked at Dooku. "Is it a trick? It could be the pirate!"

"Let's not jump to conclusions, old friend," Dooku said. "Ships break down all the time. See if you can raise them on the comm unit," he told the pilot.

But before the pilot had a chance, a frightened voice came over the speaker. "Somebody help me, please!" a girl's voice cried. "Our ship has been attacked!"

"Well now," Dooku said, his voice unruffled as he smoothly rose to stand behind the pilot. "It appears our relaxation time is over."

8

The pilot looked over at Dooku. "Answer it," Dooku said, smoothly coming up behind him. "But don't identify yourself."

"We acknowledge your transmission," the pilot said. "What is your situation?"

In answer, sobs came over the air. "I . . . I didn't think anyone would hear me. . . ."

The pilot looked up at Dooku again. "This sounds genuine."

Dooku nodded. It did sound genuine. But that didn't mean it was.

The pilot's tone was gentler now. "Tell us what happened so we can help you."

The intake of breath was so shaky they heard it clearly. "We were attacked — a space pirate. Our ship was under heavy fire. The pilot is dead. My father . . ." A sob shuddered, and then they could almost hear the child's effort to control herself. "They were taking him away. But he fought back, and they killed him."

"Identify yourself, please," the pilot said.

"I am Joli Ti Eddawan, daughter of Senator Galim

Eddawan of Tyan." The voice quavered. "The ship is failing. The warning system lights are all blinking. What should I do?"

"Who else is aboard?"

"They are all dead." The voice was small.

"That attack missed us by hours," Eero said.

"Do you know the planet Tyan?" Dooku asked.

Eero nodded. "It's a Mid-Rim planet, I think. Part of the Vvan system. I don't know the Senators there."

"Can you check on the whereabouts of Senator Eddawan?" Dooku asked. "We need to stall," he told the pilot.

"But the systems are failing —"

Dooku turned to Eero. "Now," he said, as Eero hesitated. "Go!"

Eero hurried toward the onboard computer suite. He sat down and his fingers flew over the keys.

"Hello?" the child's voice called. "I think maybe the oxygen is failing. It's in the red level. It's getting hard for me to breathe."

"Master Dooku!" the pilot exclaimed. "What should I do?"

"The order is the same," Dooku said calmly. "Stall."

"But she's suffocating!"

"Talk to her," Dooku said. "Tell her we are getting ready to save the ship."

"Joli, hang on. We are putting together a plan," the pilot said kindly. "Take very slow breaths. Lie down."

They only heard rasping breathing. "All right," Joli said. "I'm so tired. . . ."

"Oxygen deprivation," Qui-Gon murmured.

Dooku felt a spurt of annoyance. He didn't need Qui-Gon to give him a diagnosis. "Eero, do you have anything?" he called.

"Not yet! Hold on."

"Stars and planets, Master Dooku, we have to do something!" the pilot cried. "That child could die while you wait for information!"

Qui-Gon looked pale. He bit his lip, as if to prevent himself from speaking. Dooku felt very calm.

"I've got it," Eero said. "Senator Galim Eddawan of Tyan. He does have a daughter named Joli. And he was scheduled to arrive at the port station Alpha Nonce yesterday. He never arrived."

"Slowly approach the ship," Dooku told the pilot, who let out a held breath. "Keep your flank away from the center of the ship."

"It's just a small cruiser," the pilot said. "A ship like that might have some small arms, but nothing that can penetrate our shields."

"Do as I say," Dooku snapped.

"Joli? We're coming to get you," the pilot told the child.

Her voice was a mere whisper. "Good."

"Master?" Qui-Gon's voice was low. "Do you think the distress call is authentic?"

"I do not know, Padawan," Dooku said. "What do you think?"

"I feel that child is in great danger," Qui-Gon said.

Dooku raised an eyebrow at him. "I did not ask you what you felt, but what you thought." The Jedi insistence on feelings was all well and good, but Dooku preferred analysis.

"I think we should proceed carefully. We cannot ignore a distress signal," Qui-Gon said.

"Better." Dooku turned to the pilot. "Engage laser cannon tracking. Be prepared to fire."

The pilot set the controls. The silver ship dipped closer gracefully, as if initiating the first movement of a dance. The other ship sat, eerily motionless.

"Stay out of range of laser cannons," Dooku said.

"But if we don't get closer, we can't send the shuttle to board," the pilot said.

"Just do it." In another moment, Dooku would take the controls himself. He trusted the pilot's abilities more than his judgment, and he wanted to remain free to move in case the worst happened. In Dooku's experience, it often did.

Suddenly, the dead ship roared to life. It veered to the right in a burst of speed. At the same time, panels slid back on the underside of the cockpit.

"Turbolasers!" Dooku shouted. "Reverse engines!"

"Turbolasers?" the pilot asked, stunned. "That ship is too small to have that kind of firepower."

Dooku lunged forward and grabbed the controls. He

reversed the engines himself. The ship shuddered and the engines screamed in protest as they struggled to reverse at high velocity. The ship responded, zooming back out of range.

"A lesson for you, Padawan," Dooku said as the pilot took the controls again and the first turbolaser fire erupted. "Never trust anything."

The ship shook from the percussive effect of the fire, but they were out of range. Senator Blix Annon rushed into the cockpit. "What's going on?"

"We came to the aid of a distress signal," Eero said, hanging onto the back of a chair while the craft dipped and surged in evasive action. "Apparently it was a ruse."

"Apparently!" the plump Senator roared. "What are we doing answering distress calls? Who authorized this?"

"I did," Dooku said. "You put the Jedi in charge when you asked for us to escort you, Senator."

The Senator disturbed his carefully arranged hair by raking his fingers through it angrily. "I did not authorize rescue missions!" The ship lurched, and he almost fell. He snapped at the pilot, "Stop this ridiculous maneuvering. Our particle shields will protect us."

"We'll have to lower the particle shield in order to fire the laser cannons," Dooku said.

"I'm aware of that," the Senator snapped, beginning to look nervous. "Eero?"

"We also have an energy shield, to protect against turbolaser fire," Eero reassured him.

"Of course," the Senator said. "I'm aware of that, too."

"There is a difference between a particle shield and an energy field, which I'm sure you know," Dooku said as a blast shook the ship. "The energy shield will not protect against laser cannons. And we can't operate both shields simultaneously. That means that we'll have to alternate as we attack."

"Stop telling me things I know and do them," the Senator ordered. It was obvious to Dooku that despite his words, Senator Annon had no idea how his defensive and offensive systems worked. There really was no reason why he should, except that he had most likely paid a fortune for them.

Laser cannons fired as the ship bore down on them. The pilot sent them into a steep dive, and the cannonfire missed them by meters.

"They can outmaneuver us," the pilot said to Dooku. "Their ship is smaller and faster."

As if to punctuate his words, suddenly a blast hit the ship, nearly throwing them to the floor.

"What was that?" the Senator screamed.

"Direct hit," the pilot said tersely. "Another one like that and we could be in trouble."

"What are you talking about? We have a triple-armored hull! It can't be penetrated."

"Well, it has," the pilot said.

"This kind of firepower is usually reserved for capital ships," Dooku said. "The attacking craft must be custom-fitted with scaled-down versions."

Suddenly the pilot leaned over and began to frantically hit the controls. "The energy shield is malfunctioning!"

Qui-Gon's eyes flickered at his Master. This would make the difference, they knew.

"Then we'd better go on the offensive," Dooku said calmly.

"Senator, I should escort you to the safe room," Eero repeated. "Now."

The Senator looked pale. His hand fluttered and clutched at his chest. "I hardly think that's necessary —"

A blast suddenly shook the bridge, sending them flying. Dooku held on to the console and managed to stay upright, but the Senator and Eero skidded across the floor. Qui-Gon fell but anchored himself by grabbing the base of the co-pilot's seat.

Already the attacking ship was zooming to the left, ready to inflict another blow. It was nimble, darting closer and retreating, coming at them from all angles, making a tough target. The Senator's ship by contrast was now a lumbering beast. Dooku could see a plume of smoke coming from its underbelly. The intense heat was causing the armor to peel off the ship's surface in strips of gleaming metal.

"We've lost one of our laser cannons," the co-pilot reported.

"You'd better get to that safe room, Senator," Dooku said as another blast shook the ship.

The Senator didn't argue this time. Eero and Senator Annon left, staggering as they moved.

"Have you noticed something unusual, Qui-Gon?" Dooku asked his apprentice.

Qui-Gon nodded. "The ship is firing whenever we drop the particle shield in order to fire our weapons. That would take incredible reflexes on the part of whoever has the controls. Even an onboard computer couldn't obtain that kind of speed and accuracy. I've never seen anything like it."

Dooku nodded. "Neither have I."

"They've blasted the loading dock bay doors!" the pilot shouted. "They're going to get on board!"

CHAPTER No. 9

Dooku and Qui-Gon raced down the halls of the ship. When they arrived at the docking bay, the pirate ship had already landed. War droids were rolling down the ramp. It took less than a second for the droids to pinpoint their targets. Blaster fire tore up the ground in front of them and they heard it ping off the walls of the docking bay.

Dooku admired how Qui-Gon did not flinch or hesitate, but kept moving in the same fluid, graceful manner. Qui-Gon had so little of the awkwardness of adolescence. He moved swiftly and easily, his arm swinging with the motion of his lightsaber as he parried the blaster fire.

"If we can prevent the pirates from disembarking, we've got them," Dooku said as they moved. "They might decide the prize isn't worth the effort."

Suddenly the droids ejected smoke grenades from their flanks. Thick, acrid clouds rolled toward them, stinging their eyes. They kept on advancing, their eyes streaming tears.

Then a voice echoed through the thick smoke. "Please . . ."

It was the girl's voice again. "Stop — please don't

shoot. I'm here. I'm standing on the ramp. They made me. Please!" Her begging voice was full of tears and terror.

Qui-Gon stopped.

"Keep fighting!" Dooku snapped. "Don't listen!"

But Qui-Gon ran ahead and was swallowed up by the smoke. The fool was going to try to save the girl.

Angrily, Dooku rushed after him, straight into the worst of the cloud. He felt that the voice was a ruse. It had been from the start. Yet Qui-Gon's respect for the living Force would not allow for doubt. If he thought there was a chance that a child was in trouble, he wouldn't hesitate. *Curse him and his empathy,* Dooku thought, coughing from the smoke.

He took out the droids as he moved, hearing them before he saw them. The smoke thinned. He could see now that droids littered the ground. He stepped over them. Qui-Gon stood on the ramp, alone. Dooku raced up to join him and together they rushed the ship.

It was empty. Dooku strode over to the ship console. A recording rod was resting on the pilot's chair. He activated it.

"Help me, please."

Dooku shut it off.

"I'm sorry, Master." Qui-Gon looked stunned, as if he couldn't believe someone would use a child in jeopardy to get what they wanted.

"Let's go." Dooku vaulted over the pilot's seat and raced down the ramp, hearing Qui-Gon follow behind him.

Something about the situation nagged at Dooku. In the middle of a mission, he never lost his focus, or his faith that he would prevail. Why did he suddenly feel that failure was breathing on his neck as closely and persistently as Qui-Gon's footsteps behind him?

Dooku felt his heart fall when he saw that the safe room door was open. The pirate had worked extraordinarily fast. The gleaming durasteel facing was still glowing red from the blast that had blown it open.

Inside, Eero lay unconscious. His skin was blackened. Qui-Gon bent over him and began to feel for vitals.

"Not now," Dooku said. He turned and raced back out the door, down another corridor that led to the docking bay. Qui-Gon caught up to him with long strides. The ship lurched, and emergency sirens were now wailing continuously. The systems were failing.

They raced back to the loading dock. As they entered, they were just in time to see Senator Blix Annon, his hands bound with laser cuffs, being pushed inside the craft. The pirate was tall and lean, dressed in full-body armor and a plastoid helmet that concealed his face. He turned, even though they'd made no sound.

Accessing the Force, Dooku leaped. He landed on the ramp, lightsaber raised. He felt Qui-Gon land behind him. Blaster fire had already peppered the air, zinging past his ears, close and rapid. The pirate had excellent aim. Dooku had to keep the lightsaber moving in order to deflect the shots, advancing all the while. He had no doubt that he would win this battle. The pirate's eyes gleamed, the green of his iris so intense that Dooku could read it from behind the gray tint of his visor.

A dark green, shot with glints the color of flames . . . Dooku's mind lurched.

The pirate made a half turn to the left and swung out in a wide arc.

Dooku moved in an instinct so old it was automatic. He stepped away to avoid a blow that did not come.

Lorian.

Did he hear a chuckle from underneath the helmet? Dooku wasn't sure. But Lorian took advantage of that split second of hesitation, as he always had been able to, and jumped backward into the ship. The ramp closed rapidly, spilling Dooku onto the floor. He landed next to Qui-Gon and together they watched the ship roar out of the bay doors.

I will not think of this now, Dooku told himself. *If I think of Lorian, I will lose control.*

The ship was dying. Eero could be dead. The first thing to do was check on him. They ran back to the safe room, where he was struggling to rise.

"Lay back," Qui-Gon said gently. He folded a cloak and placed it beneath Eero's head.

Eero's eyes fluttered. "The Senator?"

"Gone," Dooku said.

"We have to go after them," Eero said, trying to get to his feet.

"We have more immediate problems," Dooku said. "The ship is falling apart. And you don't look so well yourself."

"I'm fine," Eero said. He stood quickly, then immediately crashed to the floor.

"Obviously," Dooku said dryly. "We'll send someone for you. In the meantime, I have a feeling the pilot needs our help."

They could feel the cruiser shudder and list to one side as they ran to the cockpit. The pilot was feverishly flipping switches. "I've got the maintenance droid working on the electrical systems, but the sublight is going."

"Where's the nearest port?" Dooku asked, striding to stand behind the pilot's seat.

"I'll check," Qui-Gon offered, moving to the onboard computer. In only a few seconds, he called out, "Voltare spaceport." He read out the coordinates. "Master, I can try to work on the sublight mainframe control."

"Do it." Dooku had no patience for the details of technology. He had already recognized that his apprentice was better at repairs than he.

"What can I do?" the pilot asked, his eyes darting nervously to the controls.

"Just keep us flying," Dooku said.

Qui-Gon released a control panel in the floor and jumped down to work on the system controls. "I think I can fuse it," he called. "If we don't push the engines, we might be able to make it."

"Push them? I'll baby them," the pilot muttered.

Qui-Gon vaulted out of the chamber and switched places with the co-pilot. "I'll keep my eye on the warning lights. You just fly," he told the pilot.

With the white-knuckled pilot gripping the controls and the steady presence of Qui-Gon in the co-pilot's chair, the ship finally limped into the Voltare spaceport.

Eero was rushed to the med clinic. The other passengers and the pilot headed for the spaceport cantina.

Dooku and Qui-Gon sat in the cockpit. Qui-Gon kept a respectful silence, realizing that his Master needed time to think.

At last, Dooku had a chance to consider what he knew.

Lorian. How could he fall so low? Once a bright Padawan, now a space pirate, preying on Senators he had once been trained to protect.

Lorian still had Force abilities, which explained the split-second timing of his laser cannon attack. It wasn't as though Dooku could have guessed, but he should have been more alert.

Enough. Jedi did not waste time on what they should have done.

What now? A momentary flame of fury burst in Dooku as he thought of his old friend on his ship, laughing at how he'd outmaneuvered him.

He controlled it. Anger was a waste of time. Action was what he needed.

Because Lorian could not win.

"We should contact the Jedi Council," Qui-Gon said.

Of course they should contact the Council. That was standard procedure. But if they contacted the Council, Dooku would have to tell them that he had no doubt that Lorian Nod was now a space pirate, and had kidnapped Senator Blix Annon right under his nose. That was something that Dooku could not do.

The Council didn't have to know yet, anyway. What

would they do? Merely tell him to proceed. They wouldn't send another Jedi team at this stage. They would trust that Dooku and Qui-Gon could handle it.

"Master?"

"Yes, Padawan," Dooku said. "We will contact the Jedi Council. All in good time." What he needed to do was find the Senator before anyone knew he was missing. "But it would be better to contact them when we know where we are going. When it comes to a kidnapping, speed is the most important factor. We are in a position to find the Senator. We must act quickly."

Dooku remembered from the data file that the pirate usually waited twenty-four hours before releasing his ransom demands.

His comlink signaled, and he saw that Yoda was trying to contact him. He placed the comlink back in his utility belt. "We should maintain comlink silence from now on," he told Qui-Gon. "All of our energies need to be focused on our search."

Qui-Gon nodded, his face showing nothing of what he felt. If he thought it was odd to maintain comlink silence, he wouldn't utter a word or even twitch an eyebrow.

"What's our first step, Master?" he asked. "Until we get a ransom demand, we don't have a place to start."

"There is always a place to start. Go over the battle in your mind, Qui-Gon. If you examine every detail, you will find at least one clue to follow. Try to remember anything that seemed out of order or doesn't make sense."

Dooku waited, watching his Padawan. Qui-Gon's gaze was remote. He could tell that his Padawan was looking out at the busy spaceport without seeing it. He was reliving the battle. Dooku already knew what his first step would be. But telling Qui-Gon would not help his Padawan learn. Qui-Gon had an excellent mind. He could analyze data rapidly and organize it to reach a conclusion.

Dooku had to wait less than a minute.

"The energy shield failed," Qui-Gon said. "And the armor plating peeled off. If the Senator really used the best security outfitters, that doesn't seem likely. The cannon fire wasn't prolonged enough to explain it."

"Good," Dooku approved.

"There must be serious flaws in the ship's armor and shields," Qui-Gon went on. "And they were able to blast through the safe room doors using conventional explosive devices."

"And what does that tell you?"

"That the Senator was lying to us, or has been cheated."

"And was the pirate lucky, or smart?"

It took Qui-Gon less than a moment to understand. "The pirate worked so fast that he had to be aware of the ship's vulnerabilities."

"Perhaps. Let's look over the data file again." Dooku reached into his travel pack and extracted the slender holofile. He accessed it and leafed through the reports of previous kidnappings. Qui-Gon read over his shoulder.

"There's a pattern," he said. "The pilots report malfunctions in security, or failures they can't explain."

"Nothing catastrophic enough to raise suspicions," Dooku noted. "First of all, the pilots and security officers are too interested in covering up their own failures. And second of all, everyone is focusing on the kidnapping, not how it occurred."

Dooku knew something else, something he would not share with his Padawan. Lorian took calculated risks. He did not like surprises. It made sense that he would somehow find a way to attack a ship that he already knew had a flawed security system.

"With all this information, what would your first step be?" he asked Qui-Gon.

"Find out where the ship was outfitted with its security devices," Qui-Gon said promptly. "Go there and investigate whether there is a connection. It will be difficult without the space pirate's identity, but maybe we'll turn up something." Qui-Gon hesitated. "There is something else. . . . I don't know how to say this."

"Just say it, Padawan."

"Something I am picking up from you," Qui-Gon said. "Anger? Something out of proportion to what happened."

There was that irritating living Force connection again. "You are mistaken, my young apprentice," Dooku snapped. "Let us focus on the matter at hand."

"Yes, Master."

Dooku would tell Qui-Gon eventually, but not yet. If

Qui-Gon knew that a former Padawan was involved, he would wonder why they weren't contacting the Temple immediately. Dooku wanted Lorian in custody before the Council found out the details. When Dooku's name was spoken throughout the Temple, it would be in the name of glory, not humiliation.

Pale and weak, Eero's head shake was surprisingly vigorous. "That's impossible," he said. "I myself arranged the security upgrades. I chose the most renowned company for vessel security — Kontag. I have an extensive file on them, I did my research. If you could get me my travel bag —" Eero pointed to a bag resting near his clothes.

Dooku handed it to him and he extracted a holofile. "Here. Just look. They are experts."

Dooku flipped through the file. It was a promotional piece that Kontag gave to prospective customers. He saw long lists of clients, and he recognized the names. Descriptions of highly technical systems, images of the factory floor. It was impressive. He himself had heard of Kontag. They were justly renowned for their excellent security systems and were often linked to the Techno Union. He couldn't imagine that there could be sabotage at one of their plants.

Nevertheless, if something looked wrong, it had to be wrong.

"Qui-Gon, see if you can look up the histories of the

ships that were attacked," he told his Padawan. "They should be in the file."

Qui-Gon accessed their data holofile and quickly flipped through it. "They were all serviced by Kontag," he said, looking up at Dooku.

"There has to be a connection," Dooku said.

Dooku stepped away from Eero's bedside and used his comlink to contact Kontag headquarters. But after questioning a number of officials, he got nowhere. He shut his comlink in disgust.

"All security information is confidential. I'm not surprised. That's how a company dealing in security has to operate."

"If they won't tell us what we need to know, what can we do?" Qui-Gon asked.

Dooku rose smoothly. "They will tell us what we need to know. But they will not know they are doing it."

CHAPTER No. 11

It was not far to the planet Pirin in the Locris sector, where the Kontag headquarters and factories were, yet even the few hours it took to get there were too many for Dooku. He had learned long ago how to conceal impatience, but he had not learned how to eliminate it.

Dooku had time to think on the way to the factory and decided that it would do them no good to demand anything. In his experience, a little subterfuge always worked better than direct confrontation.

"Do we have a plan, Master?" Qui-Gon asked, breaking the long silence.

"Follow my lead," Dooku said. "We will pose as prospective clients. The main thing we need to do is get a look at the factory floor. If there is sabotage, perhaps we can pick up something."

Dooku strode into the company offices. A recording rod flashed a holographic worker, a pretty young female. "Welcome to Kontag," the image said in a musical voice. "Please state your business and make yourself comfortable in our custom-designed seating that can be retrofitted into any cloud car."

Dooku introduced himself and Qui-Gon and said that the Jedi were interested in a large-scale project to upgrade their security devices on spacecraft. Almost instantly, a salesperson materialized from an inner office.

"I am Sasana," she said. "We're so pleased that the Jedi have thought of Kontag for their needs. We thought your order preferred to handle security internally."

"We are considering other options," Dooku said.

Sasana nodded. "Always wise. Let me show you what kind of top-notch security Kontag can provide." She handed Dooku a file identical to the one that Eero had showed them.

Dooku pretended to look through it and handed it to Qui-Gon. "Interesting. Can you show us the factory?"

Sasana's smile slipped. "That is an . . . unusual request."

Dooku's smile took the place of hers. "A deal breaker, I'm afraid. The Jedi are very particular."

He could see that the visions of a big contract were dancing in front of Sasana's eyes. "Of course," she said finally. "This way."

Sasana tried to control the pacing and thoroughness of the tour, but Dooku knew that once he got inside the factory he would see whatever he wished. They strolled down the aisles while droids flew or walked by. Panels were examined, sensor suites were worked on, and the hum of machinery made it difficult to talk. The tour ended at a prototype of a state-of-the-art speeder.

Dooku had seen enough. He told Sasana that they would be in touch and left.

As soon as they were outside, he looked at his Padawan. "Impressions?"

"Something isn't right," Qui-Gon said.

"Why is that?" Dooku asked.

"There is evidence both of prosperity and decline," Qui-Gon said. "The offices are luxurious, but there were empty work spaces, as though staff had been dismissed. The list of clients includes jobs in progress. Yet from the activity I saw, the amount of droids and material, they couldn't possibly be serving that number. And there were areas on the factory floor that indicated that machinery had once been there and had been removed."

"Excellent," Dooku said. "Conclusion?"

Qui-Gon hesitated. "They are concealing something, of that I have no doubt. But I don't know what it is."

"If the client base is correct, the work *is* being done somewhere. Just not at this factory," Dooku said. "What I see is a once-wealthy company who fell on hard times and has turned to a cheaper factory to do the work they once did. The factory here is a sham. It is not where the real work is being done."

"How can we discover the real factory?" Qui-Gon asked.

Dooku removed a sensor suite from underneath his cloak. "I think this might tell us something. Sensor suites always have a factory mark buried in their software. I took the liberty of removing it from the prototype." He drew out his datapad and inserted the suite, then tracked the information streaming across the screen. He pressed a few buttons. After only a moment, he smiled. "The Von-Alai factory planet," he said.

Von-Alai had once been a cold planet covered with snow and ice. Its inhabitants were adept at foraging a living from the icy wastes. With the introduction of factories and toxic refuse, the climate had warmed, and periodic floods devastated the countryside. Instead of halting growth, more and more factories were built, and worker housing was built on raised platforms. The owners of the factories held political power, so the decision was made to adapt to the changing climate instead of limiting toxic outflow. As a result, the native plants died, floods were common, and a once-beautiful, silvery planet was now a soggy wasteland. The air was thick and tasted metallic. Pristine snow no longer fell, only a cold rain tainted by toxins.

Qui-Gon stood on the landing platform, breathing the yellow air, silently taking in the wasted planet. "What a terrible destiny," he said. "The Alains have lost their planet."

"Beings choose their own fate," Dooku said. "They could have fought for their planet, but their indifference and their greed made them passive. There was no war here, my young apprentice. Merely beings who did not choose to fight the power that ruled them."

"Perhaps they tried and failed," Qui-Gon said quietly.

"Then they are also weak, which is worse," Dooku said dismissively. "Come."

This time, Dooku thought it better not to announce their approach. He simply walked through the factory gates. There was no security.

They entered a clamorous production facility. Grease stained the floor and accumulated in puddles. The ceiling was low and the air was dense and hot. Row after row of various workstations unfolded down the long space. Battered droids wielded servodrivers and airpumps. The workers looked half-starved and unhealthy, and Dooku saw that most of them were quite young.

"They are using children," Qui-Gon said, shocked. "Under these conditions! This violates galactic laws."

"There are many such places, unfortunately," Dooku said.

"We must do something!" Qui-Gon said, his gaze anguished as it roamed the factory. "They look as though they are ill and starving."

"Keep your focus on the mission, my young apprentice," Dooku said sharply. "We cannot save everyone in the galaxy."

"But Master —"

"Qui-Gon." Dooku only had to say his Padawan's name as a warning. Qui-Gon's mouth snapped shut.

A plump human male, his sparse hair matted with sweat and grease, came running toward them. "Excuse me, who are you? Never mind, you're trespassing, so leave."

Dooku did not move.

"Excuse me, you're not moving," the man said with a frown. "Do you want me to call security?"

"Please do," Dooku said. "Perhaps we can discuss the number of galactic laws you are breaking."

The man stepped back. "You're not Senate inspectors, are you?"

"We need information," Dooku said.

"Well, you've come to the wrong place," the man replied.

Dooku looked around the factory pleasantly. "You are busy, I see."

The man nodded warily.

"It most likely would not please your superiors if the factory was shut down under your watch."

"You have the authority to do that?"

Dooku shrugged. "Child labor. Dangerous conditions. I see grease pools on the floor, toxic compounds left open to the air. . . . There are a dozen violations I can see without even turning my head."

"What do you want? Money? We pay our bribes, but I have an emergency stash."

"As I said, merely information. Who owns the factory?" Dooku asked.

"I just send in reports. I don't know anything —"

"Who do you send reports to?" Dooku was getting impatient. He fixed his gaze on the manager.

"A company . . . I send them to a company. . . . The name of it is Caravan."

Caravan. The name of the holographic cruiser Lorian had designed. He had gone to sleep dreaming of the places he would travel in it.

That was all Dooku needed to know. He reflected on how smart and simple the scheme was. Behind the screen of a company, Lorian cut corners on security, then exploited his knowledge of a ship's vulnerability in order to attack it.

He heard a rustle behind him and turned to see Eero threading his way through the machinery toward them.

"Great. Another inspector," the manager muttered.

"I had to come," Eero said. "I followed you here — onto the transport and now to this facility. I can't bear to hear that the firm I hired to protect Senator Annon ended up being the reason he was kidnapped. I've got to help you catch the pirate and free the Senator. It's the only way."

Eero was sweaty and pale. "You look as though you need to lie down," Dooku said. Clearly, his old friend had gone to great lengths to follow them. Dooku admired his tenacity — and was suspicious of it as well.

Eero shook his head. "I've found a factory worker here who is willing to talk," he said. "He says the pirate makes regular visits here. He might know where his hideout is."

The manager had faded back, anxious to disappear.

"Let's talk to the worker," Dooku said.

He and Qui-Gon followed Eero through the aisles. No one looked at them as they walked. No doubt the workers had been punished for lagging behind, because they worked doggedly, without raising their heads.

Eero stopped suddenly and looked around. "Where did he go? He was right here." Craning his neck, he took a few steps and disappeared around a large bank of machines.

Dooku felt the rush of the Force as it warned him. He reached for his lightsaber. Qui-Gon was only a fraction of a second behind him.

Colicoid Eradicator droids wheeled around a corner and headed for them, blasters at the ready. Dooku held his lightsaber aloft.

"Master." Qui-Gon's voice was urgent. "We can't fight them. Look around."

Dooku surveyed the area around them. Child workers were everywhere here, no doubt because their smaller fingers were useful for work on sensors. If the Jedi engaged the Eradicators in battle, the blaster fire would spray the workers. They would have nowhere to hide.

Still, Dooku did not drop his lightsaber. He had no doubt that Lorian had arranged this. He knew that Jedi would not fight if it meant endangering innocent lives — especially children's lives. He would force Dooku to surrender. But he would never surrender to Lorian!

"Master." There was steel in Qui-Gon's voice. His lightsaber was already deactivated and at his side.

Dooku deactivated his lightsaber. He felt helpless rage take him over as the droids took them into custody. In his heart, he vowed revenge.

CHAPTER No. 12

Gray swirled before his eyes. Shadows that moved, that hurt as they moved, exploding inside his brain like pulses from a hot laser. Dooku tried to reach out and could not. He flexed and felt pressure at his wrists and ankles.

His vision cleared, and the shadows resolved themselves into objects. A table. A chair. He saw that his wrists and ankles were encircled by stun cuffs.

He breathed slowly, accepting the pain in his head and telling his body that it was time to heal. He called on the Force to help him, and he felt the pain ease its grip.

They had been taken by the droids, and a paralyzing agent had been introduced through a small syringe. With a painful glance down at his utility belt, he saw that his lightsaber was gone.

Qui-Gon was beside him. They were lying on a cold stone floor, the laser cuffs binding them to durasteel hoops embedded in the stone. Qui-Gon groaned and opened his eyes. His breath came out in a hiss.

"Breathe," Dooku said. "The pain will ease in a moment."

He watched as his Padawan closed his eyes again and took slow, heavy breaths. Color returned to his face. He opened his eyes. "Do you know where we are?"

"No idea." They could have been unconscious for hours and transported off Von-Alai. It didn't matter. Because Dooku had not contacted the Temple, no one had known they were on Von-Alai. There was no way to track them.

Lorian would not beat him. He vowed that it would not happen. Things didn't look good — he was bound and imprisoned at the moment — but Dooku would find his opportunity and he would use it.

"Perhaps Eero will find us," Qui-Gon said. "Or tell the Temple where we are."

"Eero is part of this," Dooku said. "He set us up."

"But he is your friend," Qui-Gon said. "And he was hurt in the invasion."

"So it seemed. Injuries can be faked. Eero was a good actor, nothing more. I was foolish not to think of it before. This should be a lesson to you, Padawan. Have as many friends as you want, but do not trust them. Believe me, I know what I am speaking of. The person who has imprisoned us was once in training with me."

"He is a Jedi?" Qui-Gon asked, shocked.

"No. He went through training but was dismissed. Never mind why. We were friends once. I am beginning to suspect that he might hold some kind of grudge against me. So there is more going on here than you know."

"You mean you knew he was the space pirate?" Qui-Gon said no more but the words hung in the air. *And you did not tell me?*

"I recognized him as he left Senator Annon's ship."

"And you think Eero is in league with him?"

"I suspect so. Betrayal is part of life, Qui-Gon, and we can't always see it coming."

Qui-Gon strained against the energy cuffs.

"That won't do anything but exhaust you," Dooku told him. "You must accept that sometimes you are in situations over which you have no control. Accept the situation and wait for your opportunity. Besides, we are farther along than we were before."

"In what way?"

"We were looking for the space pirate, and now we have found him. We'll get taken to him eventually. He won't be able to resist gloating — he never could. When we find him, we will wait for our opening, and we will not make mistakes."

Dooku closed his eyes. He did not like to feel anger and humiliation roiling inside him. He needed inner calm. He never acted out of anger.

Long minutes passed. He felt his heartbeat slow. Then he heard the swish of the doors opening.

"Old friend," Lorian said.

At the sound of his voice, rage spurted up in him again. He did not open his eyes until he had controlled it.

"I realized some time ago, Lorian, that we were never friends," Dooku said evenly.

Lorian had grown into a handsome man. He was all lean muscle. His thick gold hair was cropped short, throwing into relief the bold lines of his face and his green eyes. "You haven't changed," he said, then smiled. "Yet it's good to see you, even though it's unfortunate for me. If a Jedi had to be tracking me, I would've hoped for anyone but you. You knew me too well. Once."

"Yes," Dooku said. "I knew how you would lie and cheat to get your way."

"What is so bad about what I've done?" Lorian asked. "It was hard being in the galaxy all alone, trying to make my way. All I knew was the Temple. Did that ever occur to you, Dooku? We were raised in a bubble, and then everything I knew was taken away from me. I was forced out into the galaxy, a young boy with no Master to guide me."

"The Jedi hardly set you adrift," Dooku said. "They arranged a position for you in the Agricultural Corps."

Lorian snorted. "Tending hybrid plants on a Mid-Rim planet? Would you be satisfied with that life, after all the training we went through?"

"I had no reason to have to accept it," Dooku said. "I did not violate the Jedi Order. You did. You seem to forget that."

"I was young and made a mistake." Lorian's face hardened. "I paid dearly for it. Was I supposed to turn into a farmer? I was trained as a Jedi! So instead I went into business for myself."

"As a space pirate."

"Just temporarily. I started out kidnapping criminals, but that got risky. You'd be surprised how reluctant gangs can be to come up with the ransom. So I looked to Senators next. The only problem was, they had the best security. But what if their security wasn't as good as they thought it was? When I heard Kontag was sliding into bankruptcy, it gave me the idea. So I bought this factory and offered Kontag a deal."

"A factory that employs children." Qui-Gon's voice was flat. His gaze told Lorian that he held him in contempt.

Lorian strolled toward Qui-Gon, his face alight with curiosity. "So this is your apprentice, Dooku? Qui-Gon Jinn? Yes, I can see you in him. He is as sure of his own rightness as you are. What would you have me do, young Padawan? Fire the child workers? Many of them support families. Parents who are injured or too sick to work, or parents who have abandoned them so they are supporting their brothers and sisters. Would you have them starve?"

"I would find a better way," Qui-Gon said.

"Ah, he is unshakable. Well, I'll tell you this, young Jedi. I am planning to phase out the child labor. Improve conditions. But do you know what that takes? Money. The Jedi don't deal with credits. They don't speak of them. But the rest of us have to eat, you know."

"You are full of justifications," Qui-Gon said.

"They make the planets turn," Lorian said with a shrug. Qui-Gon's words did not sting. "Have you been to the Senate lately? It runs on justifications. I am not evil, Qui-Gon Jinn. I know this for certain. I've seen the face of true evil," Lorian said, his voice dropping. "And I have known the terror of it. So don't be too quick to judge me."

"True evil?" Dooku asked. Could Lorian mean the Sith?

Lorian turned back to him. "Yes, Dooku, I did access the Sith Holocron. I was curious. And what I saw chilled my blood and haunted my days for a long time. It haunts me still. And yet it is comforting somehow. Once you've seen true evil, you can be sure that you will never be able to fall that low."

"Don't be so sure," Dooku said. "You're a kidnapper. A criminal. How can you justify that?"

Lorian shrugged, smiling. "I need the money?"

Dooku snorted.

"Look, so what if I kidnap a few corrupt Senators for a couple of weeks? Some of them even enjoy the attention. Nobody gets hurt."

"What about us?" Dooku asked.

"I'm not going to kill you, if that's what you're wondering," Lorian said. "I'm just going to hold you until the last job is done. I'm ready to retire anyway. I'd like to return to my homeworld and start a legitimate business. I still owe some credits to Eero for setting up the whole security thing, but I have enough for myself."

"So Eero was in on your scheme from the beginning."

"Pretty much. We ran into each other on Coruscant. He was upset about his lack of a career. He was positive he'd be a Senator by now, but he didn't have enough money to really run an election. So he agreed to use his contacts in the Senate to recommend Kontag. Then once the kidnappings began, more and more Senators lined up for extra security. It was a truly brilliant plan." Lorian sighed. "Too bad it all has to end."

The doors suddenly slid open, and Eero ran toward Lorian. "Now you've done it!" he cried. Dooku could now see that outside the room was some kind of office. Laying on a console were two lightsabers.

"Calm down, Eero," Lorian said irritably. "There's no need to shout at me."

"Yes, there is!" Eero said. "The Senator is dead!"

"Dead?" Lorian looked confused. "How? He's being held in comfortable surroundings. I even sent in pastries, for galaxy's sake."

"He had a heart attack. He died instantly."

"Ah. This isn't good," Lorian said.

"No, I'd say so," Dooku said. "It's murder."

"Exactly!" Eero said. "How did you talk me into this! We'll be tried for murder!"

"Only if they catch us," Lorian said.

"I just got into this for the credits," Eero said fretfully. "I'm a politician, not a murderer!"

"Yes, this certainly changes things," Dooku said

smoothly. Eero was just as afraid of getting caught as an adult as he'd been as a young man. "You've killed a Senator. The full might of the Senate security force will come down on you. Not to mention the Jedi. They are already looking for us. This will certainly give them a reason to hurry."

"We have to get out of here!" Eero said shrilly to Lorian.

"Calm down!" Lorian barked. "Can't you see what he's doing? Shut up and let me think!"

"Don't give me orders!" Eero suddenly drew out a vibroblade. "I'm sick of it. You've bungled everything!"

"You fool!" Lorian hissed. "Put that away!"

But it was too late. Dooku summoned the Force. The vibroblade flew from Eero's unsteady hand and landed on the energy cuffs binding Dooku's wrists. The blade cut through the cuffs easily. With split-second timing, Dooku slipped out his hand before the vibroblade could injure him. He felt only a slight burn of heat.

Within seconds, he had released the other cuff and the ones binding his ankles.

Eero took one look at him and bolted out the door. Dooku reached out a hand and his lightsaber flew from the room next door into his palm.

When he turned, lightsaber activated, Lorian had Eero's vibroblade and a blaster in his hand. Dooku smiled. This time it was not a game.

Lorian backed up toward the door. Dooku saw that he meant to escape. He would try to avoid the battle if he could. Dooku leaped, blocking his exit. Lorian would not leave this room alive.

He had never forgotten Lorian, and he had never forgiven him. It was not in Dooku's nature to forgive or to forget.

"You betrayed me once, and now you've tried to make a fool of me," Dooku said.

"So glad to see you haven't changed," Lorian said, giving his vibroblade a twirl. "Can I point out again that the galaxy doesn't revolve around you, Dooku? The kidnapping wasn't personal. I didn't know you were on that ship." He grinned. "But I have to admit, I enjoyed winning."

The light mockery that danced in Lorian's eyes inflamed Dooku. The old resentment balled up in his chest, the choking rage he had felt as a boy. Now it joined the fury of a man. Dooku felt it surge, and he didn't fight it.

He was older now, and wiser. Anger no longer had the power to make him sloppy. It made him more precise.

"Talk all you want. You will never leave this room," he said with such icy control that the smile faded from Lorian's eyes.

"Let's not be so dramatic," Lorian said uneasily.

"Master give me my lightsaber!" Qui-Gon called.

The words only buzzed faintly, as if they came from a long distance away. Dooku did not need his Padawan. Qui-Gon would only get in his way. He needed to finish this alone.

Lorian had seen his intent in his eyes. Between them

now was the knowledge that Dooku would not allow him to surrender. He fired the blaster. Dooku deflected the fire easily. There was no way that Lorian could win this battle. Dooku could see the desperation in his eyes, the sweat forming on his brow. He enjoyed seeing it.

Lorian kept up a steady barrage of fire while he swung the vibroblade, using the same Jedi training he had absorbed so long ago. Dooku kept advancing. He knew perfectly well where Lorian was headed — to Qui-Gon's lightsaber. Dooku decided to speed up the process. He lunged forward and with an almost casual swipe severed the vibroblade in two. Then he whirled and kicked the blaster out of Lorian's hand.

Lorian sprang and fumbled for Qui-Gon's lightsaber. Dooku allowed him to pick it up. He had no reason to fear.

Qui-Gon cried out, but Dooku didn't hear what he said. All his focus was on Lorian now.

"Go ahead, attack me," Dooku said, holding his lightsaber at his side, letting it dangle casually. "Show me how much you've forgotten."

Lorian activated the lightsaber. Even in the midst of a battle Lorian could not win, Dooku could see the pleasure the former Jedi took in holding a lightsaber again.

He leaped at Dooku. The first strike was easily deflected. Without his connection to the Force, Lorian could not handle the weapon as he once had. Dooku enjoyed this humiliation the most. He parried Lorian's attacks, barely moving.

"Pity," Dooku said. "You were a worthy opponent once."

Now a flare of anger lit Lorian's gaze. He suddenly shifted his feet, moved unexpectedly, and came close to landing a blow.

Dooku decided it was time to stop playing with him. It was time to show him what fear was. Time to show him who the winner was.

He moved forward in perfect form, gathering the Force and molding it to his desires. His lightsaber danced. Lorian managed to evade one strike and parry the next, but it cost him. He stumbled with the effort.

"Master!"

Qui-Gon's voice cut through the heart of Dooku's concentration with the same annoying buzz.

"Master. Stop."

Qui-Gon did not shout this time. Yet his tone penetrated Dooku's concentration better than his cry had. Dooku looked over. Bound and helpless, Qui-Gon looked back.

That gaze. Dooku almost groaned aloud. He saw integrity and truth there, and he could not hide from it. He saw himself through Qui-Gon's eyes, and he could not do it. His Padawan had revealed to him what he should have known already. He could not go down this road.

He deactivated his lightsaber. Lorian took a deep, shuddering breath.

"It's over," Dooku said.

Dooku handed over Lorian and Eero to Coruscant security. He didn't speak much with Qui-Gon on the journey back. Dooku knew that there were things that needed to be said, but he wasn't sure what they were. He knew that Qui-Gon had saved him from something, and he was grateful. Yet he did not want to admit that he had come so close to violating the Jedi code he was so proud of upholding.

They walked past the rows of cruisers in the Temple landing area, the place where he had said good-bye to Lorian so long ago, for what he thought was forever.

"So what did you learn from the mission, Padawan?" he asked Qui-Gon.

"Many things," Qui-Gon answered neutrally.

"Name the most important one, then."

"That you will withhold facts from me that I need to know."

Dooku drew in a sharp breath. He did not appreciate a rebuke from his apprentice. This natural assurance of Qui-Gon's could get out of hand. What Qui-Gon needed was a little more fear of his displeasure.

"That is my decision," he answered severely. "It is not for you to question your Master."

"I am not questioning you, Master. I am answering you." Qui-Gon's gaze was steady.

Angrily, Dooku walked a few more steps. "I will tell you the lesson you should have learned." He stopped outside the landing bay doors. "Betrayal should never take you by surprise. It will come from friends and enemies alike."

He left his Padawan and walked down toward the great hall. He drank in the sounds and sights of the Temple. He was glad to be back among the Jedi. Seeing Lorian again had disturbed him greatly.

He found himself in front of the Jedi archives. Now he knew why he had felt driven here. What Lorian had left him with was envy, and he realized why.

Lorian had accessed the Sith Holocron. He had looked upon it. Maybe he had even gleaned some secrets from it.

And he wasn't even a Jedi!

Dooku had put it out of his mind for so many years, and now it had all returned — the same hunger, the same irresistible urge to know the Sith. Was it fair that a non-Jedi had glimpsed the Holocron's secrets, and Dooku, one of the greatest Jedi Knights, had not?

Dooku stood for a moment outside the archives, drinking in the silence, thinking about what lay within. Now no one could challenge his right to see it. He deserved to know, he told himself. *He deserved to see it.*

The massive doors opened, and Dooku strode in.

Dooku and Qui-Gon's final mission together had lasted two years. It had been difficult and filled with dangers. They had worked together as never before, their battle minds in perfect rhythm. They had succeeded. They returned to the Temple, weary, leaner, and older.

Dooku had not spoken of the future. Qui-Gon would now undergo the trials. They both knew he was ready. Qui-Gon waited for some parting words on the long journey home, but none came.

They passed from the landing platform into the great hallway of the Temple. Almost immediately, Qui-Gon saw a familiar form ahead and his heart lifted. Tahl had come to welcome him.

They had not seen each other in years. They walked toward each other, and they clasped each other's shoulders in their old greeting. Qui-Gon searched Tahl's striped green-and-gold eyes, needing to see that she was well and in good spirits. She nodded to let him know this was so.

"You're tired," she said.

"It was a long mission," he admitted.

He could feel Dooku waiting impatiently behind him.

They were scheduled to go straight to the Jedi Council for their report. Tahl, too, felt his Master's irritation. She nodded a quick good-bye and mouthed "later."

Qui-Gon turned back and walked in step with Dooku.

"I see your old friendship has not died, even after all these years," Dooku said.

"I trust Tahl with my life," Qui-Gon said.

Dooku was silent for the entire length of the long hallway.

"You have been an excellent Padawan, Qui-Gon," he said at last. "I could not ask for a better one. I will tell the Council this as you face the trials. But I will not tell them this: You have a flaw. This in itself is not a bad thing. Each of us has one. It is bad when we don't see it. Yet what is far worse is to see your flaw and to think it is not a flaw at all." Dooku stopped. "Perhaps it is my fault that I was never able to teach you my most important lesson."

Qui-Gon looked at his Master. The long, elegant nose, the dark hooded eyes, the pale skin. It was a face he knew intimately, but he also knew, and had known for some time, that it was a face he did not love. At first this had bothered him — until he realized he did not need to love his Master, merely learn from him. He was grateful to have a Master so strong in the Force. He had learned much.

"Your flaw is your need for connection to the living Force. Qui-Gon, the galaxy is crowded with beings. The Jedi Order is here to support you. Nevertheless you must carry the following knowledge in your heart," Dooku said. "You are always alone, and betrayal is inevitable."

Thirty-two Years Later

Qui-Gon Jinn and
Obi-Wan Kenobi

CHAPTER No. 14

Qui-Gon was the Master now, and he still remembered the lesson. It was the only one Dooku had given him that he had not heeded. Qui-Gon had come to believe that beings were more complicated than such a simple formula. And he had come to see that to live without friendship or trust was to inhabit a galaxy he did not want to live in.

Yet hadn't events in his own life proved his Master right?

Qui-Gon felt the hardness of the bench underneath him. He and Obi-Wan Kenobi were on a space cruiser crowded with beings. His eyes were closed. Obi-Wan was beside him, no doubt thinking that Qui-Gon was sleeping. Behind his closed lids, Qui-Gon imagined he could feel the speed of the ship vaulting through the stars. Every kilometer that passed in a flash carried him forward into an uncertain future.

Betrayal should never take you by surprise.

But it did. Every time.

His first apprentice, who he had nurtured, had betrayed him. Xanatos had turned to the dark side, had invaded the Temple itself, had tried to kill Yoda. Now

Xanatos was dead. He had chosen death rather than sur-render, stepping off firm ground into a toxic pool on his homeworld of Telos. Qui-Gon had leaped to prevent him even as his heart knew he was too late. He had seen the man Xanatos fall, blue eyes blazing with hatred, but at the same time, he had seen the boy he had once known, blue eyes full of eagerness, full of promise. It had cut him, made him grieve. Months had passed since the incident, and Qui-Gon felt the memory as fresh as if it had hap-pened yesterday. Had his former apprentice failed his training? Or had Qui-Gon been the one to fail?

His second Padawan, whom he also loved, had also betrayed him. Obi-Wan sat beside him now, but Qui-Gon did not feel the old harmony between them. Obi-Wan had left the Jedi Order in order to devote himself to a cause on a planet they had tried to save. Qui-Gon still remembered standing on the rocky ground of Melida/Daan, seeing something in the eyes of his apprentice he had never seen before. Defiance. Obi-Wan would not listen to Qui-Gon's order to leave. He had remained.

Obi-Wan had come to see that he had been wrong. He had done everything he could to rebuild what they'd had between them. They had begun on a long road. Trust was the goal.

Tahl's disapproving frown rose in his mind. *You are al-ways so dramatic, Qui-Gon. Obi-Wan is a boy who made a mistake. Do not hold him responsible for your failure with Xanatos.*

Was that what he was doing?

Time, you need, Yoda had advised. *That is all.*

Qui-Gon accepted that. But how much time was appropriate? When would he know? And would Obi-Wan sense his struggle and come to resent him for his stubborn heart?

Your flaw is your need for connection to the living Force.

Qui-Gon saw the truth of this. He had not completely discounted what Dooku had to say. In his daily life he tried to keep that connection in balance with his Jedi path. No attachments. He did not see this as a conflict. He saw it as a great truth — that he could love, but have no wish to possess. That he could trust, but not resent those who let him down.

Lately, that last one had been tricky.

"We're stopping for fuel," Obi-Wan said, breaking into his thoughts. They were returning from a routine training mission, and their pace was not rushed. "I'm sorry to interrupt you, Master, but do you wish to disembark? We'll be here for several hours."

Qui-Gon opened his eyes. "Where are we?"

"A planet called Junction 5. Do you know it?"

Qui-Gon shook his head. "Let's disembark," he decided. "It will do us good to stretch our legs. And I bet you could use some decent food."

"I'm fine," Obi-Wan said, bending for his pack.

Qui-Gon frowned. There it was. Once Obi-Wan would

have agreed, would have grinned at him and said, "How did you guess?" Now Obi-Wan was intent on being a "correct" Padawan. He would not admit that the days of gray, tasteless food and protein pellets were dismaying.

Maybe it wasn't a case of forgiveness at all, Qui-Gon thought as they joined the line to disembark. Maybe it was a case of missing what he'd had. He had his correct Padawan back. Now he missed the imperfect boy.

The planet of Junction 5 seemed to be a pleasant world. The capital city of Rion was built around a wide blue river. Obi-Wan and Qui-Gon took a turbolift down from the landing platform to the wide boulevard that was one of Rion's main thoroughfares.

"Every visitor must register with the local security force," Obi-Wan said, reading off a pass they had been given. "That's unusual."

"Some societies are tightly controlled," Qui-Gon said. "As the galaxy becomes more fragmented, beings are more afraid of outsiders."

They strolled down the boulevard, glad to feel the sun on their faces. But Qui-Gon had not gone more than a few steps when he felt that something was amiss.

"There is fear here," Obi-Wan said.

"Yes," Qui-Gon said. "We have an hour or so. Let's find out why." He reached for his comlink. Since Tahl had been blinded in a battle on Melida/Daan, she had made her base at the Temple and was available for research. She rarely had to access the Jedi archives; her knowledge of galactic politics was immense.

"Are you busy?" Qui-Gon asked.

Tahl's dry voice came clearly through the comlink. "Of course not, Qui-Gon. I am sitting here waiting for you to contact me so that I'll have something to do."

His smile was in his voice as he answered, "We have a stopover on the planet Junction 5. The Force is disturbed here. Can you give us an idea why?"

"We have been monitoring the situation," Tahl said. "The planet has not asked for Senate or Jedi help, but we are prepared for it. For many years Junction 5 has maintained a rivalry with its moon, Delaluna. Several years ago Junction 5 discovered that Delaluna was developing a large-scale destructive weapon, capable of wiping out cities with one blow. The citizens of Junction 5 call it the Annihilator. They live in a state of constant fear that it will be used one day."

"Have they tried to negotiate a treaty?" Qui-Gon asked.

"The problem is that Delaluna denies the existence of the weapon," Tahl said. "Talks between the two govern ments are stalled. Because of this great fear that has gripped the population, there are rumors of double agents and spies trying to undermine the government to prepare for a Delaluna invasion."

"Are they planning an invasion?"

"They say not. But we don't know. In the meantime, because of the imminent threat, the government of Junction 5 has instituted a crackdown. With the help of a security force called the Guardians, they have infiltrated every aspect of the citizens' lives. Nothing they do goes unrecorded by the government. All computer use, all comm use, is monitored. At first the citizens voluntarily gave up their privacy in the face of the great threat. But I'm afraid the Guardians have abused their power over the years. Now they really run the government. Citizens are arrested and held without trial, just for speaking out against the government. The prisons are full. The citizens live in fear. Their economy is failing, and there is even more unrest. As a result —"

"The Guardians have cracked down harder," Qui-Gon said wearily. It was a familiar scenario.

"So be careful," Tahl warned. "They don't like outsiders. You'll be watched, too. If it's a stopover, treat it that way."

"I plan to," Qui-Gon said.

"Qui-Gon? Our connection must be breaking up. I thought I heard you agree with me," Tahl said.

"Don't get used to it," Qui-Gon replied, breaking the connection. He didn't know what he'd do without Tahl. That was a connection he trusted absolutely. *No matter what Dooku told me.*

"Should we go and register now?" Obi-Wan asked.

"Let's eat first," Qui-Gon suggested. As long as they were here, he might as well gather information in case a

Jedi presence was needed at a future time. It would be easier for now if the Guardians didn't know he was here.

Besides, he never liked being told what to do.

He filled in Obi-Wan on his conversation with Tahl as they walked to the closest cantina. There weren't many selections, but Qui-Gon was able to buy some vegetable turnovers for them, along with a drink made from a native herb. As they ate, they listened to the conversations around them. The citizens spoke in hushed tones, as though they were afraid of being overheard and reported.

Qui-Gon and Obi-Wan were able to screen out background noise with the help of the Force, concentrating on a conversation at a table behind them.

"The rumor started yesterday," a soft voice said. "It could be true, or they could be covering up her death. Jaren is desperate."

"He must be careful."

"He is past that. I am afraid for them."

"She has risked everything."

"She was always willing to do that."

The voices lowered further, as if they suspected someone was trying to overhear.

"Can't we do something to help here?" Obi-Wan asked, just as quiet as everyone else.

"Our transport is scheduled to depart in less than two hours," Qui-Gon said. "No one has asked for our help. We can't solve the problems of every world in the galaxy." Even while talking and eating, Qui-Gon's gaze had continually swept the cantina. He was not particularly surprised when a security officer in a gray uniform entered and walked straight over.

"Passes, please."

"I'm afraid we don't have any," Qui-Gon said.

"All visitors are required to register at the Registry Office."

"We thought we'd eat first. Of course we'll head over that way once we're done."

"Not possible. Please follow."

The officer waited politely. Qui-Gon considered resisting, then rejected it. He wasn't on this world to make trouble, merely to observe. He stood and motioned for Obi-Wan to do the same.

They followed the officer back down the boulevard and down a side street. A large, gray building sat behind an energy wall. It was built of blocks of stone and looked like a prison.

The officer led them past the energy wall and into the building lobby. There was a small office with a sign reading REGISTRATION ONLY. The officer ushered them inside, clearly intending to make sure they followed through.

"Visitors to register," the officer said.

Qui-Gon walked forward and gave their names to a clerk. The clerk's fingers faltered when he gave their homeworld as the Jedi Temple, Coruscant.

"One moment," the clerk said, her eyes downcast.

It took more than a moment — almost ten minutes —

but the clerk finally slid two cards across the counter. "Carry these with you at all times. You are scheduled to depart in one hour, fifty-three minutes."

They walked back into the hall, their footsteps loud on the polished stone. A voice stopped them.

"It is always a pleasure to welcome Jedi to our world."

Qui-Gon felt it before he even turned, the sureness that he had heard that voice before.

The person greeting them was tall, with close-cropped blond hair that was now threaded with gray. His body was still muscular, still strong. Qui-Gon did not even need a second to remember him.

It was Lorian Nod.

Qui-Gon did not think that Lorian Nod showing up was a coincidence. The clerk must have alerted him to their presence, which was why it had taken a bit too long to obtain their identity cards.

Nod was dressed in the same gray security uniform as the officer, but with a variety of colored ribbons woven through the material on the shoulders, indicating a high rank.

It was obvious that he remembered Qui-Gon. His gaze traveled over him, and Qui-Gon remembered the way Lorian had made everything, even a life-and-death struggle, seem like a huge joke played on all of them. He had been puzzled by that as a Padawan. Now he recognized it as the defense of a man who had lost the only thing that had mattered to him, once long ago, and would never get that pain out of his heart.

"You are surprised to see me," Lorian said. "Junction 5 is my homeworld."

"I am surprised to see you out of prison," Qui-Gon said dryly.

Lorian waved a hand. "Yes, well, I was a model prisoner. I ended up helping the Coruscant security force with a number of problems they were having inside the prison, and they were grateful."

"You mean you were an informer," Qui-Gon said.

Lorian cocked his head and smiled at the Jedi. "You haven't forgiven me for what I did to your Master."

"Forgiveness is not mine to give," Qui-Gon said.

"And how is Master Dooku?" Lorian said.

"I hear he is well," Qui-Gon said. He was not in touch with his old Master. He had not expected to be. Their relationship had not been based on friendship. It had been one of teacher and student. It was natural that they should not be in each other's lives.

It would be different with Obi-Wan, Qui-Gon thought. He saw ahead to the days when Obi-Wan would be a Jedi Knight, and he would like to be part of that.

"I see that you work for the Guardians," Qui-Gon said.

"I *am* the Guardians," Lorian replied. "The old security force was helpless in the face of the great threat, so I proposed a new force. The leader of Junction 5 asked me to be the head of it."

Qui-Gon was surprised. A former criminal was head of planetary security?

"You see, I am completely rehabilitated. So, what are you doing on Junction 5?" Lorian asked, smoothly changing the subject.

"A stopover," Qui-Gon said.

"And this is your Padawan?"

"Obi-Wan Kenobi, Lorian Nod," Qui-Gon said.

"Did you know I was once a Padawan as well?" Lorian asked Obi-Wan, who shook his head. "I left the Order."

Obi-Wan could not conceal the surprise on his face. Qui-Gon could read him like a datascreen. Someone else had left the Order? So he was not alone. And then the apprehension came as Obi-Wan realized — *if I had left, is this what I would have become?*

"At first I thought it a terrible punishment, but now I see it was meant to be," Lorian continued. "Well, this has been delightful, but I have duties to perform. Enjoy your journey. I suggest you be on time for your transport. Security here must be very tight, to protect us. If you overstay your pass, there could be some trouble for you."

Qui-Gon knew they were being threatened. "Jedi are used to trouble," he said.

Lorian gave him a keen glance. "I have a brilliant idea. Because of my old ties to the Jedi, I will help you. I'll provide you with escorts to make sure you arrive at the transport on time. The streets of Rion can be confusing to the traveler."

"That is not necessary," Qui-Gon said.

"Now, now, don't thank me," Lorian said firmly. "It is done."

The two security officers followed behind the Jedi as they made their way back to the landing platform.

"Lorian Nod seemed pretty insistent that we leave," Obi-Wan said.

"I never like being shown to the exit," Qui-Gon replied.

Obi-Wan caught his meaning and grinned. "Should we lose them?"

"In a minute. Do you notice something, Padawan? Since we arrived, more and more security officers are out on the streets. Somehow I doubt this has anything to do with us."

"Do you think there is an alert?" Obi-Wan asked.

Qui-Gon turned to the officers behind them. "Rion is a beautiful city."

"Yes, we are proud of our homeworld," one of them said stiffly.

"The citizens seem happy."

"They know they inhabit the best planet in the galaxy," he said.

"Tell me," Qui-Gon went on pleasantly, "it appears you have much crime in your capital city."

The officer stiffened. "There is no crime in Rion."

"Then why do I see so many security officers?" Qui-Gon asked.

"Extraordinary circumstances," he answered, frowning. "There is an Outstanding Threat to Order. An enemy of the state has escaped from prison. Cilia Dil is very dangerous. The security officers are looking for her."

"I see," said Qui-Gon. "What was her crime?"

"I have told you enough," the officer snapped. "Hurry

or you'll miss your transport. If that happens, you'll be arrested."

"You arrest people for being late?" Qui-Gon asked mildly.

"Don't be ridiculous. For overstaying your pass."

Ahead, a large utility vehicle was unloading cargo from a repulsorlift platform. Traffic backed up behind the large vehicle, and pedestrians were stepping into the street in order to get by. Qui-Gon indicated the mess ahead to Obi-Wan with just a shift of his eyes. Obi-Wan didn't nod or show any sign, but Qui-Gon knew that his apprentice was ready.

As they came up toward the vehicle, Qui-Gon used the Force to disturb a precariously stacked column of boxes. The produce spilled over into the street while the workers shouted and cursed.

The pedestrians stepped on the produce, mashing it into the pavement and making the workers shout at them angrily. Qui-Gon and Obi-Wan leaped. The Force propelled them over the mess, the citizens, and the workers, leaving the security officers behind.

They hit the street and ran, dodging between pedestrians who quickly jumped out of the way. They turned onto a smaller, quiet street, then another and another. Soon Qui-Gon was sure they had lost their pursuers.

"Now what?" Obi-Wan asked.

"I say we find Cilia Dil," Qui-Gon said. "It's likely she would have many interesting things to tell us."

"But the entire army of the Guardians are looking for her," Obi-Wan said. "How can we find her?"

"Good point, my young apprentice," Qui-Gon said. "In such cases, it becomes more reasonable to create a situation where *she* finds *us*."

It didn't take them long to find out more about Cilia Dil. Although no one would speak to them directly, afraid they were spies, conversations were easily overheard, and everyone was talking about the escaped rebel. Qui-Gon was not surprised to discover that the conversation they'd overheard that morning had been about Cilia, and that Jaren was her husband.

He lived in the middle of the city, in a large building with many apartments. The Jedi paused, pretending to look in a store window at the end of the block.

"There is surveillance on the roof," Obi-Wan said. "But they are only watching the front door. We can come from behind, go down the alley, and find a side window."

"That is exactly what they want you to do," Qui-Gon said. "Look again."

It took only a moment for Obi-Wan to scan the area again. He looked crestfallen, as if he'd deeply disappointed Qui-Gon. "I saw a flash in a window next door overlooking the alley. Electro-binoculars. They are watching the alley, too. I'm sorry, Master."

It wasn't like Obi-Wan to apologize for a wrong call. He

had always absorbed Qui-Gon's small lessons without comment. Then he never made the mistake again.

How can I give him back his confidence? Qui-Gon wondered.

"What do you propose?" Obi-Wan asked.

"Do you have any ideas?" Qui-Gon asked, prodding gently.

But Obi-Wan wouldn't venture another plan. His lips pressed together, and he shook his head. He was afraid to disappoint him again, Qui-Gon saw.

Qui-Gon buried his sigh in an exhaltation of breath as he glanced up at the sky. "It's late. The end of a working day. I say we seek our advantage in routine."

"Workers and families will be coming home," Obi-Wan said.

"So let's see what develops," Qui-Gon agreed.

At first it was just a trickle of passersby, but within minutes the street was crowded with people on their way home. Repulsorlift transports jammed with workers paused to open their doors and more beings spilled out on the walkways.

Qui-Gon and Obi-Wan loitered outside a shop near Jaren Dil's building. They didn't have to wait long. Soon a mother and a group of children came down the street. The mother carried a sack of food and various other bags as her children ran around her legs, shrieking with joy at being released from school. They paused for a moment at the entrance ramp outside the building. One of the small children, daydreaming, almost got swept up in the sea of people on the sidewalk. Qui-Gon quickly moved forward and picked him up. He joined the group at the ramp. Obi-Wan quickly followed.

"Tyler," the mother scolded. "How naughty." She reached for the boy while she fumbled for her entrance card. Obi-Wan lifted several sacks from her arms to help.

"Allow me to carry him," Qui-Gon said, making a face at the boy. "We've made friends."

The mother thanked him gratefully while inserting her entrance card. Obi-Wan juggled the bags and put a hand on another boy's shoulder. To an observer, it would appear that the Jedi were simply two other members of the family.

They helped the mother to her door and said good-bye to the children. There was no turbolift, and they had to climb the stairs to the top floor. Qui-Gon knocked politely on the door, which was opened by a tall man with sad eyes.

"Are you Jaren Dil?" Qui-Gon asked.

He nodded warily.

"We have come about your wife," Qui-Gon said.

Jaren Dil blocked the doorway. Despite the fact that he was almost a meter shorter than Qui-Gon and so thin he was almost gaunt, he did not seem intimidated. "I know nothing about my wife's escape."

"We wish to help," Qui-Gon said.

A twisted smile touched Jaren's lips, then disappeared. "You would be surprised," he said softly, "how often we have heard those words. They always say they wish to help."

"We are Jedi," Qui-Gon said, showing the hilt of his lightsaber. "Not Guardians."

"I know you are not Guardians," Jaren said. "But I don't know who you are, or who your friends are. I am expecting to be arrested at any moment. My crime is being married to Cilia Dil and not betraying her."

"I would like you to get a message to her," Qui-Gon said.

"I have not seen Cilia since she was arrested. She was allowed no visitors. I don't know where —"

Qui-Gon interrupted. "Tell her the Jedi want to help." Qui-Gon reached for Jaren's comlink, hooked onto his belt. He entered his code. "I have given you a way to contact me. We will meet her anywhere she wants."

Jaren said nothing. They walked away, down the stairs. They did not hear the door close until they were out of sight.

"He didn't trust us," Obi-Wan said.

"He would be foolish if he did. He is used to betrayal."

"So why do you think she'll contact us?" Obi-Wan asked.

"Because in desperate times, the desperate seek out those who offer help. The fact that we are Jedi is on our side. They will discuss it. Then she will contact us."

"You seem sure of it," Obi-Wan said. "How do you know?"

"They have no one else to turn to," Qui-Gon said.

It was lucky for them that a full-scale hunt was on for Cilia, so catching the Jedi was not a high priority. That was why the guards around Jaren's house did not notice as they left. Qui-Gon and Obi-Wan walked the streets, reluctant to sit in a café or even on a bench in a park. They needed to be mobile in case they were spotted. Security officers patrolled, but they were able to avoid being stopped.

Dusk fell like a purple curtain. The shadows lengthened and turned deep blue. With the cover of darkness, they felt a bit more secure. Qui-Gon was beginning to wonder if he was wrong, and Cilia would not contact them. Then, the comlink signaled.

"What is it that you think you can do for me?" a female voice asked.

"Whatever it is you need," Qui-Gon answered.

There was a short silence. "I'm going to hold you to that."

Qui-Gon marveled that Cilia could sound humorous after escaping from a notorious prison. "Tell me where and when we can meet you."

Cilia named a small pedestrian bridge that crossed the river and the hour of midnight. Qui-Gon and Obi-Wan had passed the bridge several times that day in their looping journey around the city. They were tired later that night as they walked there and stood at the edge, out of reach of the glowlights. The city was silent. Most of the citizens were home. They heard only the soft lapping of the river against the stones of the bridge.

Yet Qui-Gon felt that Cilia was near, close enough to hear them.

"You may as well trust us," he said out loud.

A reply came from underneath the bridge. "It's a little early in our relationship."

Qui-Gon realized that Cilia must be in a small boat, but he did not bend over to look.

"Well, you've come to meet us," Qui-Gon said. "I'll take that as a sign."

A dark shape suddenly vaulted out from underneath the bridge and landed close to them. Cilia was dressed in a waterproof suit, and her short hair was slicked back behind her ears. She was tiny and slender. The bones of her wrists looked as delicate as a bird's. The slash of her cheekbones created hollows in her face. Her eyes were the dark blue of a river. Underneath them were dark circles, marks of her suffering.

"Why do you want to help me?" she asked.

"Lorian Nod was once a Jedi in training," Qui-Gon said. "He has created trouble for this world. Let's say the Jedi owe the people of Junction 5 their support."

"He was training to be a Jedi? That could explain things. He seems to know things . . . things he couldn't know, even by surveillance." Cilia pushed away a lock of hair that had fallen onto her forehead. "I have a plan. Some Jedi help would be welcome. It's dangerous, though."

"I would expect so," Qui-Gon said.

"I've put together a team to travel to Delaluna," Cilia said. "Our idea is to break into the Ministry of Defense and Offense in order to steal the plans of the Annihilator. We can't rely on our government to take action — obviously they are paralyzed with fear — and they are afraid action will lead to reaction. Yet if we get the plans, perhaps we can discover a way to defend ourselves from the weapon. And if the citizens again feel free, the repressive government will have no reason to exist, and we can refashion a more just society."

"*Dangerous* is putting it mildly," Qui-Gon said. "I'd add difficult and foolhardy to that."

Cilia put one foot on the railing, ready to vault back down into the river.

"Count us in," Qui-Gon said.

They spent the night in Cilia's hiding place, a safe house on the outskirts of the city. Cilia disappeared into an inner room, and Obi-Wan and Qui-Gon were left to share floor space in a small, bare room painted a surprising pink. They laid out their sleeprolls and settled down on the hard floor.

"Master," Obi-Wan murmured, "should we contact the Council?"

"Why?" Qui-Gon asked.

"Well, we're about to break into another planet's government building and steal state secrets," Obi-Wan said. "Master Windu can get touchy about things like that."

"Precisely why we shouldn't bother him. I'll speak to the Council after the mission is over. Don't worry, Obi-Wan. The Council doesn't have to know every move we make, nor do they want to. You worry too much."

"You don't know what I'm thinking all the time," Obi-Wan growled.

"Not all the time," Qui-Gon said. "But at this moment I do."

"What am I thinking, then?"

"You are thinking about that turnover at the cantina and wishing you'd had time to finish it."

Obi-Wan groaned and turned his face into his sleep-roll. "I'm too hungry to argue. I'm going to sleep."

Qui-Gon smiled into the darkness. Obi-Wan's breathing grew steady, and soon he had dropped off into sleep.

Qui-Gon rolled himself tighter in his blanket and stared at the ceiling. Flakes of paint had peeled off the surface, revealing a dark undercoat somewhere between brown and green. He had forged his own path apart from Dooku, but there were some lessons he had kept. A certain independence from the Council made things easier on a mission. Afterward was another story. Obi-Wan was right. The Council would not be happy they had joined Cilia's raid.

Qui-Gon was impressed by the organization of the resistance. Cilia had arranged transport for the team and had even obtained worker identification tags from the Defense and Offense Ministry of Delaluna.

"You must have been planning this for some time," Qui-Gon said.

Cilia nodded as she climbed into the transport. "I planned it from prison. I was tired of peaceful protest. We need to strike one blow — and win."

"How did you communicate with your group?" Qui-Gon asked. "Your husband said you had no visitors in prison."

"The resistance has many friends," Cilia said, setting

the coordinates. "There was a guard at the Guardian prison who smuggled in messages. He had joined the Guardians and became disillusioned. He said there were others like him. That's why I have hope."

The transport lifted off and streaked toward the moon of Delaluna. The journey wasn't long, and soon they had exited the craft at the landing platform outside the capital city of Levan.

Cilia had kept the group small. In addition to the Jedi, there was a security expert named Stephin and a weapons specialist named Aeran.

Their passes worked, which eliminated one of Qui-Gon's worries. The ministry was a bustling workplace, and they didn't attract any attention as they walked through the halls.

Cilia had memorized the layout. She led them onto a turbolift and down a long hallway into a separate wing of the building.

"I got the layout from a friend," she told Qui-Gon. "There are also those on Delaluna who don't like this situation. She passed along the blueprints to Stephin."

They reached the Weapons Development wing. Cilia stopped. She swiped her identification card, but the doors did not open.

"Stephin?"

"It's supposed to be card entry only," Stephin said, stepping forward.

Qui-Gon had taken in the situation in a glance. "It's now retinal and daily code."

"Daily code?" Stephin shook his head. "We're sunk. I can crack it but it would take hours. Plus I don't have a mainframe on me."

Qui-Gon admired Cilia's coolness. She did not show her exasperation. Her skin seemed to tighten over the sharp cheekbones. "We're here," she said. "I'm not leaving without those plans. We have to find another way."

"We don't necessarily have to get into the secure wing ourselves," Qui-Gon said. "Not if we can get in through a computer."

Cilia looked at him, interested. "How?"

"We need to go to the only one who has access to all files and documents in the system," Qui-Gon answered.

"The director," Cilia supplied. "Of course. I don't know what kind of security he has, though."

"Let's find out." Qui-Gon indicated that Cilia lead the way.

They returned to the main wing of the Ministry. The director's office was behind a frosted panel. An assistant sat behind a desk. Beyond him was another door.

"No doubt the assistant has a panic button if we try to force our way in," Stephin said. "And we have no way of knowing if the director is in his office or not."

They walked on, anxious to avoid attention. At the end of the hallway, Cilia frowned. "We have to get both of them out of that office. We need a diversion."

"I think we can supply that," Qui-Gon said, beckoning to Obi-Wan.

They turned off from the others. Ahead, down a side hallway, Qui-Gon had already seen what he was looking for — the office for Internal Security.

"What are we doing?" Obi-Wan murmured.

"You are a new employee," Qui-Gon told him. "Just be as confusing as possible and leave the rest to me."

What Qui-Gon had found was that security officers in corporations or government offices were all basically the same in one respect. They were all afraid of being dismissed.

He strode in and scanned the room. Security screens lined two walls, and the tech equipment panel was as big as the room. Just as he'd hoped, there was only one technician there. A burly man rose from where he was idly playing a one-handed game of sabaac.

"Thought I'd walk him over," Qui-Gon said, indicating Obi-Wan. "Your new employee. Clearance from the top."

"Whoa, hang on, slick," the burly man said. "Just who do you think you are?"

"Security consultant from Constant Industries," Qui-Gon said. "I guess the director didn't tell you I was hired."

The burly man looked a little uncertain. "Credentials?"

Qui-Gon flashed his identification badge. "Look it up on the computer. Or call the director's office."

"I'm a secured weapons surveillance expert," Obi-Wan explained. "Trained at the tech institute? I'm supposed to monitor the in-house systems and coordinate the armed-response team."

"Wait a second. I'm the head of in-house systems," the burly man said.

Obi-Wan shrugged and looked at Qui-Gon.

"Not anymore, I guess," Qui-Gon said. "Let's take a look at what you've got here."

"Now, wait a second," the man said. "You can't come in here and —"

"Right, right, you're absolutely right. The security drill is coming up. We're supposed to monitor that closely."

"We're not scheduled for a security drill."

"You'd better check that," Obi-Wan said. "There was a test system override and a cross-tech flareup with a monitor glitch that fried the subsystem. Let me show you." He leaned over the panel.

"You can't touch that!"

"Wait a second. You didn't set the security drill?" Qui-Gon took out his comlink. "I'd better notify the director."

"Wait, wait."

"I can take over," Obi-Wan said.

"I'll do it!" the man said, roughly pushing Obi-Wan aside. He made several keystrokes, and an alarm sounded.

"Security drill," a voice announced. "Please go to your stations."

"Come on," Qui-Gon said to Obi-Wan. "We'd better monitor the procedure. It's bound to be sloppy."

"But wait!" the burly man called. "What are your names?"

Crowds of beings had spilled out into the hallways. Obviously used to security drills, they continued to chat as they moved slowly down the halls to the exits. Obi-Wan and Qui-Gon threaded through the crowd.

Cilia was watching for them anxiously. "I'm assuming you did that," she said.

"Yes. We'd better move forward or we'll look suspicious. Has anyone come out of the director's office?"

"Not yet."

"There they are," Obi-Wan said quietly.

The door to the director's office opened, and several people filed out and headed for the exit.

"Come on, let's go," Qui-Gon said.

They left the stream of people and quickly slipped into the room.

"I'd guess you have about three minutes or less," Qui-Gon told Stephin.

Stephin didn't take the time to reply, but immediately entered the director's office and accessed his computer. He clicked keys quickly.

"Can you crack it?" Cilia asked.

"Hang on." Stephin's fingers flew. Qui-Gon was fairly adept at cracking computer security, but even he couldn't begin to follow Stephin's code.

"I'm into his personal files," Stephin said. "Nothing out

of the ordinary . . . whoa! Hold that transmission. I found the Annihilator file." He clicked a few keys. "This is strange. You'd think there'd be a number of files, but there's only one." A holofile appeared. "It's subtitled Mis-information," he said. "Odd, don't you think?"

Cilia and Qui-Gon bent in front of Stephin to read the file while Aeran peered over their heads. Obi-Wan stood lookout.

Qui-Gon and Cilia's eyes met. "Do you think it's true?" she whispered.

"I think so," Qui-Gon said. "It's incredible, but it makes sense."

"I don't believe this," Aeran said slowly.

"What?" Stephin asked impatiently. Their heads were blocking the file.

"You know that awesome weapon capable of wiping out our entire civilization?" Cilia asked. "It doesn't exist. There is no Annihilator."

"What? How can that be?" Stephin exclaimed.

"This is a record of correspondence between the di-rector and the ruler of Delaluna," Cilia explained as she scanned the file. "The Ministry Director has tracked a ru mor that Delaluna has developed a fearsome weapon. He admits this is untrue, but suggests they take advantage of the rumor."

"Why quash it?" Qui-Gon said. "It will help them with security if planets think they are too strong to attack."

"They know that Junction 5 once looked at them and thought of colonization," Aeran filled in. "So why should they let their enemy know they are vulnerable?"

Cilia jackknifed erect, her dark eyes blazing. "Do you see what this means? If there's no weapon, there's no need for the Guardians to exist! We won't have to fight them, they'll simply disband!"

Qui-Gon was about to speak, but Obi-Wan signaled him.

"Guard droids approaching," he said. "Someone must know we're here."

"We must escape," Qui-Gon told the others. "If we are captured here, the news might never get out."

Cilia reached for her blaster. "We're ready."

CHAPTER No. **17**

The droids on Delaluna were small, airborne, and quick, equipped with paralyzing darts and blasters. Qui-Gon did not recognize the model, but within seconds he had estimated velocity, path, and blaster range.

He needed to protect the group. Cilia and Aeran were adept and fast, but Stephin was obviously not trained with weapons. Still, Qui-Gon also had to make sure they had proof that the Annihilator didn't exist.

Obi-Wan must have had the same thought. He deflected blaster fire from the droids and leaped in front of Qui-Gon as three droids headed for him. Qui-Gon reached over and hit "copy" on the computer console. FILE COPIED flashed on screen. He reached out to extract the disk just as two droids headed toward him, flanking him on either side.

Obi-Wan moved before Qui-Gon could react. He jumped in the midst of the heavy attack, his lightsaber a constant arc of movement as he deflected the barrage of blaster fire. Qui-Gon grabbed the disk and tucked it into his utility belt, then gave a backhanded sweep with his lightsaber that cut a droid in two and sent it crashing in a battered heap of twisted metal and fused circuits.

Stephin had taken refuge behind a desk and emerged to spray blaster fire in a random pattern that only occasionally hit an airborne droid. Cilia and Aeran worked back-to-back, covering each other as they moved toward the door, trusting the Jedi to take care of the bulk of the droids.

Obi-Wan launched himself over a desk, striking out at one droid with a carefully aimed kick that sent it crashing against the wall, splitting it into pieces. At the same time he swiped through another. Qui-Gon took out two droids with one swift stroke and moved to get Stephin as Cilia and Aeran took out two new droids buzzing through the doorway.

"There they are!" the security officer shouted, pointing at Obi-Wan and Qui-Gon.

"Time to go, Padawan," Qui-Gon said. He pushed Stephin in front of him, turning to deflect a new spray of blaster fire from behind.

Obi-Wan moved to take out a droid and landed in the doorway, lightsaber slashing. The security officer stepped back, unwilling to engage. He expected the droids to do his fighting for him.

With a Force push, Qui-Gon sent the officer flying. The man slumped on the floor, dazed and unwilling to get up.

"There's an emergency exit this way," Cilia said, jerking her chin toward a side corridor. "It should be open, since we're in the middle of a drill."

Workers were beginning to stream back into the building. They took advantage of the confusion by separating and melting into the crowd. Qui-Gon and Obi-Wan followed Cilia as her slight figure weaved through the crowd, heading purposefully toward the exit.

They stepped out. The sky had darkened and was threatening a hard rain. A few drops pattered against the building.

Ahead in the dark sky Qui-Gon saw a light. It was moving fast, traveling far beneath the clouds.

"Security vehicle," he said tersely. "We'd better get to our ship."

Because of the rain, many pedestrians had moved to the sheltered walkways that hugged the buildings and shops. A large canopy overhead blocked out the downpour as it began. Qui-Gon and the others hurried along this path.

The overhang protected him from the ship above. The crowds acted as further camouflage. Their ship wasn't far. They climbed inside and Cilia started up the engines. They shot into the dark sky, streaking toward Junction 5.

Cilia let out a whoop of triumph. "We did it. We did it!"

Stephin shook his head. "I still can't believe there is no Annihilator."

"This is all we need to end this reign of terror," Cilia said. "We can go straight to Minister Ciran Ern and tell him that the Annihilator is a hoax. He'll disband the Guardians."

"We can free our citizens from fear and terror," Aeran said. "It is almost too much to believe."

"I suggest that before you do anything, you ask a most important question," Qui-Gon said. "Rumors don't arise out of the air. If the Annihilator is a fabrication, who made it up?"

The others paused.

"Does it matter who made it up?" Aeran asked.

"I'm afraid it matters very much," Qui-Gon said softly. "Let me ask another question. When did Lorian Nod come to power?"

"Eight years ago," Cilia answered.

"And the memos dated back —"

Cilia's face changed. The happy flush drained away, and she grew pale. "Nine years," she said.

"And who benefited the most from the Annihilator?"

Cilia's face hardened. "The Guardians. They seized control." She looked at him shrewdly. "So you think Lorian Nod created the rumor."

Qui-Gon nodded. "I do. It is a bloodless grab for power. Create something the population fears enough, and they will hand over control to whoever appears with a solution."

"Yes, at first Lorian appeared to be our protector," Aeran said.

"Ciran Ern is said to be a puppet of Lorian Nod's," Cilia said.

"What makes you think that he would allow the truth to get out?" Qui-Gon asked. "He has much to fear from

Lorian, and Lorian will certainly find out. I guarantee that you will be denounced as crazy or as a spy, and be thrown into prison again."

"So what can we do?" Stephin asked.

"You must bypass the rulers and tell the people," Qui-Gon said.

"Impossible," Aeran said. "The Guardians control all communications."

"That is what makes it possible," Qui-Gon replied after a moment's pause. "We must get control of that system. We must discover how it works and where it is."

"I already know how it works," Stephin said. "I was part of the original design team. The central control is within the Guardians compound. It's impossible to break in."

Cilia nodded. "The Guardian compound is way out of my league. The security is flawless."

"No security is flawless," Qui-Gon said. "I can guarantee one way to get inside."

The others looked at him. Obi-Wan smiled. He already knew the answer.

"We must get arrested," Qui-Gon said.

With Guardians swarming all over the city, it was not hard for Cilia, Stephin, Qui-Gon, and Obi-Wan to get arrested. They were all wanted. Aeran had no outstanding warrant, but as a weapons specialist, her skills were no longer needed. Promising to alert the resistance to be on the lookout for a big announcement, she left them.

Qui-Gon suggested that in order to conserve time, they simply do what Lorian expected them to do. Cilia pretended to try to see her husband. She and Stephin tried to sneak into Jaren's apartment by going over rooftops. Within moments they were surrounded by undercover Guardians. As Jaren watched, white-faced, his wife was once again led away to prison.

Once they were sure that Cilia and Stephin had been captured, Qui-Gon and Obi-Wan headed to the part of the city known to be a meeting ground for the resistance. They were picked up almost immediately.

Qui-Gon and Obi-Wan were led to the Guardian compound, where they were ushered into a holding cell. Cilia and Stephin were already there.

"Guardian Nod will be informed of your capture after

the planet-wide address," the officer said, engaging the security lock. The durasteel door clanged shut.

"What planet-wide address?" Obi-Wan asked Cilia and Stephin.

"Nod gives them from time to time," Cilia said. "It usually has to do with some new alert about the Annihilator that requires stricter security measures. Now we know what a fake that is."

"How is the address broadcast?" Qui-Gon asked.

"It goes out simultaneously on all data and vid screens all over the planet," Stephin explained. "There's a studio right here in the Guardian compound."

"Could you patch into the feed with this?" Qui-Gon asked, holding up the disk that contained the information they'd seen on Delaluna.

Stephin nodded. "Absolutely. But we'd have to get out of here and into a secure area. All the studio feed lines run though the central information console."

"Speaking of which, how *are* we going to get out of here?" Cilia asked.

"That won't be hard," Qui-Gon said, pulling aside his tunic and revealing his lightsaber.

"But weren't you searched?" Stephin asked.

"We have ways of diverting attention," Obi-Wan told them. He and Qui-Gon had used the Force to distract the guards from their lightsabers during the search.

The Jedi ignited their lightsabers and sank them into the durasteel door. The metal melted and peeled back, glowing orange, and they stepped through the hole. The corridor was empty, but they could see by a blinking light that a silent alarm had been tripped.

Qui-Gon looked back at the gaping hole. "You lose the element of surprise, but it's a quick escape."

"We'll have to move fast," Cilia said.

They ran down the corridor. Cilia and Stephin both knew the complex well, and they led them through a maze of back hallways to the central computer station. It was empty, but a high-security lock was on the door. Through the glass, they could see a row of vidscreens. Lorian Nod had already begun his address.

"How long will it take you to bypass the circuits and patch through into the feed?" Qui-Gon asked.

"Hard to say," Stephin answered. "Three minutes. Maybe four."

"The alarm will go off as soon as we break in," Qui-Gon said. "They'll be able to pinpoint our location then. Just do the best you can. We'll take care of whatever comes along."

Cilia and Stephin nodded to tell them they were ready. Qui-Gon and Obi-Wan used their lightsabers to break through the door. Immediately, a red light began to pulse. As they walked through the doorway, another indicator light began to blink.

Now they could hear Lorian Nod's voice. ". . . And it is with great reluctance that I stand before you now. Yet even with bad news we can gain comfort from the fact that we are strong and able to protect ourselves from the great threat. . . ."

Stephin hurried to the console. His fingers began to fly. Qui-Gon gave him the disk and turned to face the doorway, lightsaber at the ready.

It took only seconds before the droids came. Qui-Gon had no doubt that they would be followed by armed guards. Obi-Wan sprang forward, his lightsaber flashing. They moved in the same rhythm, ready to cover each other, knowing when the other would go on the offense. It was a flow Qui-Gon remembered, when he knew what his apprentice would do before Obi-Wan did it. The Force surged around them, gathering so that it felt like heat and light, making every move easy.

Within seconds, battered and smoking droids littered the floor.

"Stars and galaxies," Cilia breathed. She had not had time to draw her own blaster.

"Three more minutes," Stephin muttered.

". . . We are tracking a group of spies who are planning to undermine our society, striking at our security itself. Thanks to the Guardians, we will be safe from them and their plans. . . ."

"I'm entering the disk codes now," Stephin said.

"The information will come onscreen," Cilia said. "But will the citizens believe it?"

"Leave on the audio feed," Obi-Wan told Stephin.

Obi-Wan spoke the words crisply, like an order. He did

not glance at Qui-Gon. He was totally focused on the moment, on the problem at hand.

Qui-Gon felt a surge of satisfaction. It was as though Obi-Wan had taken a step on a journey back to him.

Puzzled, Stephin nodded.

Qui-Gon heard the sound of boots thudding in the hallway. "Take no lives," he told Obi-Wan. If they could accomplish this without loss of life, it would be a good day.

". . . that a new blast potential of the Annihilator has been discovered . . ."

The security officers thundered in, blasters pinging, electrojabbers swinging.

"Stay behind us!" Qui-Gon shouted to Cilia, who now was ready to fight and had stepped forward.

The blaster fire was furious. Qui-Gon jumped and twisted, trying to be everywhere at once. Obi-Wan moved to protect Stephin. The guards were well trained for battle. They kept constantly on the move, using sophisticated flanking maneuvers. Qui-Gon realized that Lorian's Temple training had come in handy.

Still, the security officers were not Jedi. Qui-Gon and Obi-Wan could keep them at bay. He heard more boots thundering down the hallway and the distinctive whirr of oncoming droids.

Yes, they could keep the attackers at bay, but if more and more arrived, how long would it be before blaster fire got through?

Qui-Gon could see that the same thought had occurred to Obi-Wan. His Padawan did not flag, but a renewed burst of energy sent him in a spinning arc. He deflected blaster fire at the same time he destroyed two oncoming droids with a well-placed kick.

Then the moment Qui-Gon was waiting for occurred.

The image of Lorian Nod fuzzed and broke into shattered pieces. A memo flashed onscreen.

Stephin had been able to keep the audio feed open. The voice of Lorian Nod boomed out.

"What is that? What is happening? Get that off the screen!"

MISINFORMATION REGARDING "ANNIHILATOR"

The memo title could be read clearly. More information streamed across the stream as the holofile unfolded.

WE KNOW NOT HOW OR WHY THIS RUMOR BEGAN . . .

"Get that off the screen!" Lorian shouted. "Don't you see what it is, you fools? It's a lie!"

The focus of the security officers wavered. Qui-Gon saw their eyes drift to the screen. They tried to keep fighting and keep track of what was flashing.

Another voice came through the feed. "This says that there is no Annihilator!"

It must have been another officer in the studio who had blurted it out.

"It's a trick," Lorian said. "Spies . . ."

"It's an official document from Delaluna," another voice said. "Look at the code seal."

The officers had all stopped fighting. They stared at

the screen in disbelief. Whoever was programming the droids had stopped. They stopped in midair.

"Let's go," Qui-Gon said to Obi-Wan.

They raced out into the corridor. Following directions Stephin had given them, they ran to the studio and burst through the door.

Lorian's face was dark with rage. "You are under arrest, Jedi!"

"I believe you are mistaken," Qui-Gon said calmly. "We are arresting *you*."

"That arrest can only be ordered by the president himself!" Lorian snapped. "Guards! Take these Jedi away."

A guard across the room lowered his comlink slowly. "The arrest order has come through," he said. "I am to detain you, Lorian Nod, by order of Minister Ciran Ern."

The color slowly drained from Lorian's face. He tried to smile, but it looked as though it cost him a great deal of effort.

Looking at Qui-Gon and Obi-Wan, he shrugged. "How strange life is," he said. "The galaxy is so immense, but I can't get away from the Jedi. They have destroyed my life once again."

Lorian Nod was in prison, awaiting trial. Cilia was no longer an underground hero, but a public one, able to walk the streets with her husband. The Guardians had fallen into disarray and the minister had promised to disband them.

It was time for the Jedi to leave.

Qui-Gon waited at the landing platform with Obi-Wan. He remembered arriving on this planet while worrying about what was to come with his apprentice. It was true that he missed that pure trust, that lack of shadows between them. He had seen the flaws in Obi-Wan, and the flaws in himself. He had seen where their flaws could rub up against each other and create fissures in their relations, cracking them open like a groundquake could split the very core of a planet.

Yet there was something to be gained from that, Qui-Gon thought. Now their relationship could truly begin, for they had seen the worst of it and they had both decided that what they wanted, the most important thing, was to go on. There had been no betrayal. Qui-Gon knew Dooku was wrong — he was not alone.

"The idea to leave the audio feed open was a good one," he told Obi-Wan. "Lorian was trapped by his denials."

"I thought he might say something incriminating," Obi-Wan said.

"You ordered Stephin to do it," Qui-Gon said. "You did not check with me. You did not even look at me."

"I am sorry, Master —"

"It was the right thing to do."

Qui-Gon saw the flash of pleasure in Obi-Wan's eyes.

He is no longer afraid of displeasing me, Qui-Gon thought. *Good.*

"Shall we board?" Qui-Gon asked.

"Of course, Master." Obi-Wan paused and looked longingly at a food court. "But can we eat first?" He grinned. "I'm still thinking about that turnover."

Qui-Gon laughed. Yes, his Padawan was back. And the boy was back, too. Now they could begin again.

He had not known the Jedi cruiser to Naboo was taking him on what would turn out to be his final mission with Qui-Gon. Yet they both had understood that the time was coming when Qui-Gon would recommend him for the trials. Obi-Wan knew he was ready, but he was not yet prepared to leave his Master. He was anxious to be independent, but he was reluctant to come out from the protection of his alliance with Qui-Gon. It was not apprehension that kept him there, but loyalty. Friendship. Love.

They had spoken more on that trip than they had ever spoken before. Qui-Gon had been in a rare talkative mood, and they had remembered old missions, old acquaintances. They had laughed over the exploits of Didi Oddo, the friend who was always in trouble. They had remembered the loyal brothers, Guerra and Paxxi, now heads of large families on their homeworld of Phindar. From time to time a shadow would cross Qui-Gon's face and Obi-Wan knew he was thinking of Tahl, who he had loved. Tahl had been killed during a mission to New Apsolon despite their intense efforts to find and save her.

The pilot dimmed the lights for sleep. Still Qui-Gon and

Obi-Wan did not move. They sat on their chairs, reluctant to move to the sleep area. A silence fell between them, as companionable as always. In the dark silence, Obi-Wan had asked the question that had been in his mind for months.

"Master, can you tell me something I am lacking? Something I cannot see that I need to work on?"

He could not see Qui-Gon's face clearly now. "Do you mean a flaw, Padawan?"

"Yes. You have told me that I worry too much, and I've tried to work on that."

"Ah. You mean you've worried about worrying too much?" Qui-Gon's voice was light. He was teasing him.

"I can be impatient with living beings, too. I know that. And sometimes, I'm a little too confident of my abilities, perhaps."

Now Qui-Gon's tone was serious. "These things are true, Obi-Wan, but they are not flaws. I have seen how hard you have worked. I've seen what you can accomplish."

"Then what is my flaw?" Obi-Wan asked.

There came a silence so long that Obi-Wan wondered if Qui-Gon had fallen asleep. Then his voice rose out of the darkness, soft and deep.

"You will be a great Jedi Knight, Obi-Wan Kenobi. I know that with every breath, with every beat of my heart. You will make me proud I was there at your beginnings. If you do have a flaw, perhaps it is simply this: You wish to please me too much."

Twenty-three Years Later

Obi-Wan Kenobi and
Anakin Skywalker

Obi-Wan had never understood the meaning of Qui-Gon's words. He had meant to ask him after the mission was over. He had puzzled over the words, forgotten them, remembered them again, pushed them away only to have them reappear in his mind.

And now, they haunted him.

The Clone Wars had begun. The galaxy had fractured and the Republic was threatening to split apart. They had discovered that the former Jedi, Count Dooku, was leading the Separatists. Many Jedi had lost their lives on Geonosis six months earlier. The tragedy of that battle infused the Temple, made every Jedi walk with a heavy step. Their vision had been clouded for so long. They realized this, yet their vision did not clear. It was as though a dark curtain was draped over the Temple.

And something had changed within Anakin Skywalker. Something that made Obi-Wan uneasy. And now a worry had been pushed to the forefront of his mind — had his love for Qui-Gon blinded him to the faults in Anakin for too long?

The uneasiness he felt about Anakin, the sense of dull dread that had the power to wake him up from a deep sleep, now had a partner: the conviction that it was too late to do anything about it.

His Master could not have foreseen all that had taken place. Yet he had placed a sure finger on the spot that was most vulnerable in Obi-Wan. Obi-Wan had opened his heart to Anakin because of Qui-Gon's belief that Anakin was the chosen one. Had he tried too hard? Had he overlooked what he should not have overlooked?

Love had never blinded Qui-Gon. But it has blinded me.

There was too great a distance between him and Anakin now, at a time when he needed to keep his Padawan even closer than before. Every instinct told him that Anakin had been profoundly changed while they were apart before the Battle of Geonosis. He knew that Anakin had been to Tatooine and he knew Anakin's mother was dead. He knew that a bond had grown between Anakin and the brilliant Senator Padmé Amidala.

He sensed that some of the change was for the better. Some not. It was as if Anakin had grown harder — and more secretive. One thing Obi-Wan saw clearly: Anakin had lost his boyishness. He was a man now.

Whatever the changes were, they did not bring Anakin peace. Obi-Wan sensed his Padawan's restlessness, his impatience. He saw that Anakin no longer felt the same sense of peace from the Temple. He always wanted to be moving. He always wanted to be somewhere else.

Obi-Wan stood in the doorway of the Map Room of the Temple, watching Anakin. This was a place Anakin came when his mind was restless. For some reason his Padawan found it calming to set dozens of holographic planets spinning while voices intoned their details: geography, language, government, customs. Out of the chaos, Anakin would distinguish one voice. Then he would trace another, then another, until he could clearly hear each voice amid the babble.

Anakin had grown quite adept at this game, Obi-Wan saw. Holograms whirled around his head like angry insects. The voices were a confusing blur to Obi-Wan. He couldn't imagine why someone would find peace during this. As he watched, Anakin lifted a finger and added another planet to the mix.

"Anakin."

Anakin did not turn. Most beings would. Instead he lifted a hand. One by one the planet holograms disappeared, the voices cut off until the last solitary voice was silenced. Obi-Wan noted that it had been intoning the precious metals of Naboo. Anakin stood and turned. Obi-Wan could see that Anakin was still not used to his new artificial hand. He hugged that arm a little closer to his body. The sight tore at Obi-Wan's heart.

"Master."

"Master Yoda has requested our presence."

"A mission?"

"I do not know."

Over the past weeks there had been much to do, too much to plan — too many battles. The Jedi Council held constant strategy sessions. It was necessary to carefully place the Jedi where they were most needed. Systems and planets were now vulnerable, and many were highly strategic. The Separatists were gaining new planets with a combination of coercion and force. Supreme Chancellor Palpatine pledged to help planets loyal to the Republic.

"You go to the Map Room when you are troubled by something," Obi-Wan said as they walked. "Do you want to talk about it?"

Anakin made a restless gesture. "What is the good of talking?"

"It can be very good," Obi-Wan said gently. "Anakin, I see that the past months have marked you. I am your Master. I am here to help you in any way I can."

He could see his Padawan only in profile, but Anakin's mouth tightened. "I have seen things I wish I had not seen. I did not think so many Jedi could die. I did not think a once-great Jedi Master could fall so far."

"Count Dooku's fall has troubled us all," Obi-Wan acknowledged. "Now we have a great and powerful enemy." His thoughts turned to his battle with Dooku. He had never met such power in battle before. He had never come up against something that had completely overpowered him. Even meeting the Sith Lord who had killed Qui-Gon had not been the same. If only Qui-Gon were alive, to give them insights into Dooku. Now Obi-Wan thought back and wondered why Qui-Gon had never spoken of his Master. He would never know that, either.

He would have liked more time to talk to Anakin, but they drew up in front of the reception chamber where Yoda had asked them to convene. Obi-Wan stepped forward to access the door but it slid open before he could. Yoda was always a step ahead of him.

Yet Yoda had a more significant surprise. He stood in the middle of the room with Lorian Nod. Lorian was older, his hair completely silver now. He wasn't as lean, but his body still looked strong. Dressed in a cloak of veda cloth, he looked more like a successful businessman than a soldier, but it was unmistakably Lorian Nod.

"What is he doing here?" Obi-Wan barked. He was seldom, if ever, rude. But lately he hadn't had the time to hide his feelings. Anakin was not the only one who had developed impatience.

"To help the Jedi, Lorian Nod has come," Yoda said.

"Really," Obi-Wan said, strolling in. "Are you offering to set up your own security force, Nod?"

Lorian bowed his head slightly, as if he had expected Obi-Wan's jibe and accepted it as his due. "I knew I would meet skepticism if I came here," he said. "All I can say is that I admit I have not operated within galactic laws during some periods of my life. Yet now, when things are so serious, I find that I must return to my beginnings. I wish to help the Jedi."

"And how do you think you can do that?" Obi-Wan asked.

Yoda blinked at Obi-Wan. It was just a blink. But it told him that his tone was not appreciated.

"Ruler of Junction 5, Lorian Nod is," he said.

Again, Obi-Wan was surprised. "How did you manage that? The last time I saw you, you were about to go to prison for a very long time."

"I did go to prison for a very long time," Lorian answered. "Then I got out."

"And you seized power," Obi-Wan said, disgusted.

"Obi-Wan." Yoda's voice had a quality Obi-Wan recognized, something he thought of as durasteel sheathed in ice.

Chastised like a youngling, Obi-Wan indicated that Lorian should go on.

"I was elected," Lorian said. "When I got out of prison, things had not changed much on Junction 5. Because Delaluna had allowed them to believe that they possessed the Annihilator, the great distrust between them had not diminished. The population still lived in a climate of fear. I suggested that I be an envoy to Delaluna and open talks between us. As the one who caused the worst of the trouble, I could be the one to stop it."

Obi-Wan crossed his arms, waiting.

"I would have failed," Lorian said, "if it wasn't for Samish Kash. He had recently been elected as ruler of Delaluna. He, too, believed that the mistrust between two such close planets was harmful to them both. He believed that open trade and travel between Junction 5 and Delaluna would benefit everyone. So we sat down at a table and began to talk. We reached an agreement, and trade began. Borders were opened. We formed a partnership with the Bezim and Vicondor systems to build the Station 88 Spaceport. Both our worlds thrived and prospered. Because of the success of our plan, I was elected leader of Junction 5 three years later. I have ruled during a peaceful time. Our two little worlds were overlooked by the powers in the galaxy. In the Senate, we were one tiny voice among many. And now everything has changed."

"The systems of Junction 5 and Delaluna, found they are. Crucial to the success of the Separatists, they have become," Yoda said.

"The Station 88 Spaceport," Lorian Nod explained. "We are a gateway to the Mid-Rim systems."

Yoda lifted a hand, and a holographic map appeared. Junction 5 and Delaluna were illuminated. "If Junction 5 and Delaluna fall under Separatist control, fall Bezim and Vicondor will," he said. "Control they will a vast portion of the Mid-Rim systems."

"Count Dooku knows this very well," Lorian said. "He has contacted me. So far he has tried flattery and bribes to sway me to the Separatists, and I have lied and said I was leaning that way. Officially Samish Kash and I have not allied ourselves with either the Separatists or the Republic. I am not sure which way Kash is leaning, but I know that I have kept my own allegiances hidden. If Dooku knew I was loyal to the Republic, he could use force against my world — something I desperately wish to avoid. And I want to keep the Station 88 Spaceport as a strategic base for the Republic."

Obi-Wan nodded. He was interested now. He could see how important the tiny worlds of Junction 5 and Delaluna had become.

"Why not just declare your allegiance in the Senate?" Anakin asked. "They would send troops to protect you."

"Spread thin, the clone troops have become," Yoda said. "Our last option, that would be. A better way, Lorian has suggested."

"You may not be aware of this, Obi-Wan, but Dooku and I were friends during Temple training," Lorian said. "We had a falling out, but that was many years ago. I'm not sure if Dooku trusts me, but he needs me. It also makes sense to him that I would want to join the Separatists."

"It makes sense to me, too," Obi-Wan said. "Why don't you?"

"Because I have seen how making beings afraid or angry is the best way to make a power grab," Lorian said. "The Separatists have a point — the Senate has become a corrupt place where the needs of smaller systems go unheard. They have taken this resentment and used it as a screen for their own ends. Who are Dooku's main backers? That is where I look. The Commerce Guilds. The Trade Federation. The Corporate Alliance. The InterGalactic Bank Clan. What do they all have in common but wealth, and the desire for more power? This movement is a cover for greed." Lorian shook his head. "I am no longer able to access the Force as I did before. But I don't need the Force to show me that this road is a road to darkness."

Yoda bowed his head in agreement. Obi-Wan agreed as well. He just didn't like hearing this from Lorian Nod.

"Master Yoda, you had my first loyalty, and you have it still," Lorian said. "I have done things in my life that I know were wrong, but I am here to do right. I am here to serve the Jedi."

"What do you propose?" Obi-Wan asked. He wasn't interested in Lorian's avowals. He was only interested in what he would do.

"Dooku has called a meeting," Lorian said. "I have indicated to him that Samish Kash is leaning toward the Republic. He thinks he needs me to persuade or strong-arm Samish into the Separatist camp. Also at the meeting will be the rulers of Bezim and Vicondor. Dooku has proposed this as a friendly meeting at his villa on the world of Null."

"I've heard of this world," Obi-Wan said. "Dooku has its leader in his pocket. It was one of the first to join the Separatists."

"Although he proposed this as a neutral place to meet, obviously we are on his territory," Lorian agreed. "I have agreed to come, as have Samish Kash and the rulers of Vicondor and Bezim. We have a strong alliance among us. We have always acted as one. Dooku is hoping that I will help him convince the others to join the Separatists."

"And what do you propose?" Obi-Wan asked.

"I am not proposing anything except that I will attend this meeting as a spy, and hope to bring back useful information," Lorian said. "If the Jedi give me a specific task, I will perform it."

"Request we do that while we confer you wait here," Yoda said.

He accessed the door to an interior chamber. Obi-Wan and Anakin followed.

"I don't trust him," Obi-Wan said as soon as the doors closed behind them.

"Ask for your trust I do not," Yoda said. "Asking for your help I am. No matter his past, help us Lorian Nod can."

"He could have been sent here by Dooku," Obi-Wan said. "This could be a trick."

"Unlikely it is," Yoda said.

"Qui-Gon told me that Dooku and Lorian Nod were bitter enemies," Obi-Wan said. "Why would Dooku trust him now?"

"He said that Dooku didn't trust him," Anakin said. "But he needs him. Alliances are seldom based on trust, only need."

Yoda nodded. "Wise, your Padawan is. Think I do that best for this assignment, you are. If refuse you must, understand I will."

"What is it you wish us to do?"

"Travel to Null. This thread you must follow. Discover if Lorian is truthful. On this, the downfall of Dooku could depend."

Null was a world of forests and mountains. It had no large cities, only small mountain villages, each so fiercely individualistic that attempts at alliances had always failed. There was a planet-wide government and a system of laws, but crimes tended to be solved among villagers according to an ancient tradition of fierce, swift retaliation that left no witnesses.

It was a perfect world for Dooku's hidden retreat. The villagers had a fierce sense of privacy and kept his comings and goings secret.

As Obi-Wan guided the small cruiser to the landing platform, he deliberately looped around the coordinates of Dooku's villa. Dooku had taken over the cliffside dwelling of a monarch who had reigned hundreds of standard years before. It had originally been built of stone, but Dooku had faced it in durasteel that was the exact gray of the mountain cliffs. The durasteel had been treated so that it did not gleam. It seemed to suck in light rather than reflect it. If Obi-Wan had not been looking for the villa, he would have missed it.

Obi-Wan guided the cruiser to the landing platform.

They stood, feeling a bit odd in their clothes. They were dressed as hunters, with thick short cloaks made of animal skins. Hunting was the only tourist trade that Null supported. The mountains were full of wild beasts prized for their skins, especially the wily laroon. They disembarked, feeling the cold wind against their faces like a slap.

"We're scheduled to rendezvous with Nod in the Spade Forest," Obi-Wan told Anakin as he paid a fee to an attendant droid to keep the cruiser at the platform. "We should avoid being seen with him, even though we're in disguise. We have time to check into the inn at the village."

Anakin nodded as he slung his pack over his shoulder. "Just don't make me shoot anything," he said.

Obi-Wan grinned. The small joke brought back the days when everything was easy between them.

They were below the tree line, so the path ran through a heavy forest. The mountains rose around them, stabbing the thin air with their snowy, jagged peaks. The landing platform had been built into the largest mountain, which rose into the clouds. It was under this mountain that the village crouched.

The thick trees cleared as they walked down the mountain and the roofs of the village appeared. The buildings were made of stone and wood and were only a few stories tall.

Narrow streets wound through the cluster of buildings. The villagers seemed to rely on a sturdy native animal, the bellock, for transportation. Obi-Wan saw only a few speeders parked in yards.

Then they turned a corner and saw a cluster of gleaming speeders in front of a tall stone building, and they knew they had found the inn. Obi-Wan and Anakin entered, keeping their hoods on. The interior lobby was scattered with seating areas made of plush materials. A fireplace twenty meters tall held a huge blazing fire that chased away the damp chill. Various beings sat around the fire, some consulting datapads, others drinking tea. By the look of their clothes, Obi-Wan guessed they were outsiders, most likely aides to the rulers of the four planets. In a dark corner a hunter sat, covered in skins, an awesome array of weapons at his feet. His bored gaze seemed to regard the sleek, sophisticated beings with contempt.

"He's got enough weapons to bring down a capital ship, let alone a laroon," Anakin remarked in a low voice.

Obi-Wan's gaze traveled up the fireplace. The wall was fashioned of jagged stones from the mountain, fitted together in intricate patterns. He could see no evidence of mortar or joinery, but each stone nestled against each other in what must have been perfect balance.

The innkeeper smiled as he greeted Obi-Wan and Anakin. He was obviously a native Null. They were tall humanoids, easily a meter taller than Obi-Wan and Anakin. The men wore heavy beards, which they braided, and both men and women dressed in animal skins and thigh-length boots. "I see you are admiring the stonework of the inn," he said. "It is a native art. One pull of the keystone and the whole wall comes tumbling down."

"And which is the keystone?" Obi-Wan asked.

"Ah, that is the maker's secret," the innkeeper said. He noted their traveling clothes and sacks. "Always glad to welcome our hunters to the inn," he said. "As you can see, we have important guests, very important guests. But we do not neglect our regular trade." He pushed the data register toward Obi-Wan.

"What's going on here?" Obi-Wan asked, bending forward to sign the register. "I didn't realize Null was now on the tourist track."

The innkeeper leaned closer. "A very high-level meeting, I believe. Don't know what it's about. But I expect more of these meetings in the future. So book early or you'll be out of luck!"

"We'll be sure to." Obi-Wan pushed the register back along with the credits to pay for a room.

A young woman sat in a small chair tucked against the wall. He had not noticed her before, and would not have noticed her if a flicker of recognition didn't jolt him. He could not place her, but he felt he knew her. She was slender, dressed in a dark green tunic the color of the leaves outside. A matching headwrap covered her hair. He had met thousands of beings all over the galaxy, and though his memory was excellent, it was hard to remember everyone. Or maybe she just reminded him of someone. . . .

He turned. "Anakin, do you recognize that woman in green, sitting against the wall?"

"What woman?" Anakin asked.

There was a flicker of green, and the door of the inn closed. Obi-Wan filed the woman away in his mind to investigate later. He didn't like it when something nagged at him.

The hunter warmed his hands at the fire, picked up his weapons, and rumbled to the door. The native Null workers rolled their eyes after he had passed, clearly considering him an overly armed amateur.

"Come on," Obi-Wan said. "Let's find our room. It's almost time to meet Lorian."

First they stowed their gear in their room, a small one tucked under the eaves of the roof. Obviously they were not among those "important guests" the innkeeper had mentioned.

They walked out into the village street and toward the path that led into the forest. Obi-Wan called up the prearranged coordinates on his datapad. They would meet not far from the village in a forest clearing that Lorian had already determined was secluded but not difficult to reach.

As they reached the edge of the village, they saw a villager running down the mountain path. The thud of his panicked footsteps came to them clearly.

"Sound the alarm!" he shouted. "There's been a murder! Samish Kash has been assassinated!"

Three blasts of a horn sounded as Obi-Wan and Anakin raced up the trail. They found Samish Kash lying a few meters off the main path. Villagers crowded around him, and a speeder arrived. Samish Kash was loaded onto it. Obi-Wan saw the blaster wound near his heart. He was a young man with curly dark hair, dressed in a plain tunic. As far as Obi-Wan could tell, he was unarmed.

Lorian Nod stood by, his face full of sorrow. He acknowledged the Jedi with a glance, then leaped aboard the speeder that held the body of Kash.

Obi-Wan saw the young woman in green turn away. Her shoulders were shaking. The hunter with the impressive arsenal put a hand underneath her elbow.

"An aide to Samish Kash," one of the villagers whispered. "She found his body."

Then we will most definitely need to talk to her, Obi-Wan thought. He watched the young woman and the hunter. Now his mind was clicking. They were arguing in a way that told him they were not strangers. Obi-Wan began to drift closer, hoping to overhear. But they kept moving away from the circle of villagers, the woman trying to get away from the hunter while still talking to him.

As she made an abrupt move to turn away, her hood fell back, and he saw that she had blond hair, braided tightly and coiled around her head. Then he caught a flash of wide blue eyes. The hunter spoke urgently in her ear.

"It's Floria and Dane," Obi-Wan said.

Anakin looked where Obi-Wan had indicated. "The brother and sister bounty hunters we met on Ragoon-6? How can you be sure? It was so long ago."

"Look carefully."

Anakin studied them. "You're right. What are bounty hunters doing here?"

"Exactly what I'd like to find out."

The two Jedi moved quickly through the crowd. Floria and Dane had now moved well away from the commotion.

"If you had done what you were supposed to —" Dane was saying.

"So you're saying it's my fault?" Floria's voice was choked with anger and tears. "You always —"

"You never —" Dane stopped talking as Obi-Wan and Anakin walked up.

"I must confess I never expected to see you again," Obi-Wan said.

Floria and Dane stared at them for a long moment.

"Black holes and novas, it's the Jedi," Dane said. Now Obi-Wan could see his blue eyes, so much like Floria's. "What are you two doing here?"

"Which is exactly what I want to know about you two," Obi-Wan said, steering them farther away from the others, and underneath the trees. "Who are you hunting? Are you involved in the death of Samish Kash?"

"No!" Dane exclaimed. "We're his bodyguards!"

"Obviously, you are doing an excellent job," Anakin said. Floria burst into tears.

"Bounty hunting was getting too dangerous," Dane said, handing his sister a cloth to wipe her tears. "There were so many of us out there that all honor was lost. Some were using truly cutthroat techniques."

"I've seen a few," Obi-Wan concurred.

"So we decided to become bodyguards. It's simpler. Samish Kash hired us a couple of months ago for protection. He didn't want the usual big goons or guard droids. He didn't want anyone to know. So Floria posed as an aide, and I just used disguises. Then this meeting was called. Samish told us to be especially careful. He's the glue that keeps the Station 88 Spaceport alliance together. Without him, it would fall apart. He's the one everyone trusts. So he thought if some group wanted to take over the spaceport, they'd go for him first." Dane looked distraught. "Then instead of staying in my sight, or Floria's, the way he promised, he disappeared. I followed, and . . ."

"You found him dead?"

"Lying there," Dane said. "Shot in the heart."

"And you saw nothing?"

"What does it matter?" Floria asked them. She had wiped her tears away and her face was pale. "He's dead."

Dane shook his head. "I was too late." He looked off into the trees. "I should have —" Dane stopped abruptly and squinted into the trees.

Without another word, Dane took off. He raced to his swoop hovering nearby in suspended mode. He leaped aboard and took off.

"Come on, Anakin," Obi-Wan said, spurting forward. "We'll have to follow on foot."

The trees were dense here, and Obi-Wan could see ahead that Dane was having trouble navigating between the trunks. He had to continually slow his speed. He was obviously chasing someone ahead of him on a swoop, which appeared and disappeared through the trees.

They gained on Dane, hurtling through the spaces between the trees. When they were meters away, Anakin leaped high to grab a tree branch. Using the momentum, he swung forward and dropped neatly on the back of Dane's swoop. The swoop lurched and careened toward a massive tree trunk. Dane let out a piercing yell. Calmly, Anakin stood on the back of the swoop and leaned forward to grab the controls. He steered away from the trunk, circled, and came back to Obi-Wan.

"He'll get away!" Dane cried.

"Who?" Obi-Wan asked.

"I don't know! But I think he killed Kash!" Dane cried

breathlessly. "I don't know where I know him from, but I know him. He's a bounty hunter."

"Mind if we take over?" Obi-Wan asked Dane.

He jumped off the swoop. "Be my guest. Just be careful with my swoop!" he yelled after them as Anakin sent the engines screaming to maximum.

Suddenly, Obi-Wan wished he were driving.

The suspect glanced back once and saw they were still following. He chose a difficult route through the trees. The narrow spaces were hard to get through, especially at high speeds. Anakin flipped the swoop, turning constantly to come at the openings at the best angle, never slackening speed. He crashed through leaves and branches. They were gaining, but Obi-Wan was positive he'd lose an arm or an ear in the process.

"Do you think you could slow down?" Obi-Wan yelled over the sound of cracking twigs and the screaming engines.

"And miss all the fun?" Anakin asked, executing a quick left turn, flipping the swoop, then flipping it back again. Obi-Wan tried to find his breath.

The ground was rising sharply. The suspect pushed his speed. He careened through two trees, lost control, and the swoop flipped over and scraped the side of the next tree, sending the swoop spinning wildly. The assassin leaped off a moment before the swoop crashed into a large tree. He hit the ground and ran.

"We've got him now," Anakin said, gunning the engine.

Obi-Wan caught a blur of large brown spots speckling the tree trunks as they zoomed fast. A *strange mold?* he wondered. The spots had hairs that waved in the air like legs. They were legs, he realized.

Spiders. About the size of a small rodent animal. Obi-Wan had read about them in his briefing notes on the journey to Null. They weren't poisonous, but one had to watch out for their —

"Anakin, watch out!"

Ahead the sunlight had just caught the silky threads of the giant web slung between the trees. The swoop hit it head-on. The web did not break. The reclumi species of spider had a web so strong it could stop a moving vehicle.

It did.

The swoop boomeranged backward, crashed into the tree trunk behind them, then shot forward again, caught in the sticky web. The ropy tendrils clung to Obi-Wan's skin and hair and caught in his mouth. When he tried to pull the skin of the web off him, it stuck to his fingers.

"Aarrgh!" Anakin gave a strangled cry as he tried to pull the web off his face.

Obi-Wan managed to unsheathe his lightsaber and activate it. He cut a swath through the web, creating a hole. He dropped to the forest floor. Anakin landed next to him. Tendrils of the web still stuck to their skin, and they tried to get it off, but it stuck to them like a strong glue. The swoop hung above them while a spider with legs more than a meter long scuttled across a tree trunk to see what it had caught

Meanwhile, the assassin had disappeared. They would have to track him.

They ran quickly through the trees, snaking through the forest. The assassin had doubled back. After tracking him for a kilometer, Obi-Wan suspected that he was heading back toward the village.

They came out on another path that veered downhill sharply. Through the trees they could occasionally see the rooftops of the village. The path ended at the outskirts of the village, near some outbuildings. A large stone building had a side parking area for speeders.

"Anakin, stop. There he is."

The assassin was moving from shadow to shadow across the street. They could see now that he was a human male, dressed in dark clothing and wearing a helmet with a brim that that shadowed his face.

Then Lorian Nod appeared from the back pathway to the mountain. He was walking quickly and didn't notice the Jedi.

"He's meeting Lorian," Anakin said.

Suddenly the street came alive with villagers. They surged forward, shouting in their native language and brandishing blasters and the native weapon, a sharp blade atop a thick wooden pole. The assassin melted back into the shadows.

The villagers rushed down the street. Lorian was lost in the midst of them. Suddenly, Obi-Wan saw that Floria and Dane were being herded near the front of the crowd. Their hands were bound in lasercuffs in front of them.

Dane caught sight of Obi-Wan. "They think we killed Samish!" he shouted. "Help us!"

Floria and Dane were carried along with the crowd. The villagers surged into the stone building like one giant moving beast. The street was suddenly empty. Lorian had vanished.

"Should we try to find him?" Anakin asked.

Obi-Wan sighed. "He's not going anywhere. And we'd better see what's happening with Floria and Dane."

They walked into the building. It was a basic prison, but the security wasn't sophisticated. The cell was a small room in a corner with a durasteel door and a basic security coded lock. There were no official guards, no datascreens, no evidence of record-keeping or comm devices. Obviously this was used as a holding cell until the villagers decided on their own brand of justice.

The locals sat around a massive wooden table, drinking tea and grog and arguing. Obi-Wan stepped forward.

"We would like to see our friends."

"They are our prisoners." This was growled from the largest villager who sat at the head of the table.

Obi-Wan dug into the bag at his side and threw the skin of a laroon on the table. They had brought skins and furs with them to cover their identities.

"We would like to see our friends," he repeated.

The fur of the laroon was inspected with knowing fingers. Then the villager nodded. He rose slowly, ambled to the lock, and keyed in the security code. The door slid open.

Dane was pacing in the cell. Floria sat quietly on the one chair provided. The door slid shut behind the Jedi.

"Thank the stars you are here. They are going to kill us," Dane said.

"Don't be so dramatic," Floria said. "You don't know that."

"Let me think. They just debated on whether to use

blasters or do it slowly by lowering us into a laroon den. What's your conclusion?" Dane asked fiercely.

"They can't just kill us without a trial," Floria said. Obi-Wan noted that she had regained the color in her cheeks. Floria had been a pretty girl. Now she was a beautiful woman.

"Of course they can! This is Null! They don't bother with trials here!" Dane cried.

"Floria, Dane, if you could stop arguing for a moment," Obi-Wan said, holding up a hand. "Do they have evidence against you?"

"I found the body, and Dane came up right after," Floria said.

"In other words, they don't need evidence," Dane said. "We're outlanders. We were in the vicinity. That's all they need to know." He slumped against the wall of the bare cell and drifted down until he was sitting on the floor.

"We will protect you from the villagers," Obi-Wan said. "But you must help us."

"You were Kash's bodyguards," Anakin said. "You must have a few likely suspects. Who would have hired that assassin?"

Floria shook her head. Dane shrugged.

"No one and everyone," Dane said. "He didn't have any particular enemies. He had brought prosperity and peace to his people. But with this Separatist thing, everything changes. It could have been Dooku himself. It could have been one of the other members of the alliance, Telamarch or Uziel, if they wanted to control the alliance."

"You didn't mention Lorian Nod," Anakin said.

"Him too, I guess." Dane looked gloomy. "I don't trust anybody."

"Not Lorian Nod," Floria spoke up. "They started the alliance together."

Obi-Wan crouched down near Dane. "Dane, you said the assassin looked familiar. You have to remember where you met him."

Dane buried his head in his hands. "Floria and I have been all over the galaxy. I've met so many beings. He's one in a line of awful ones. I really need to retire." He looked up. "Hey, how's my swoop, by the way? Is it safe?"

Obi-Wan and Anakin exchanged a glance.

"Well, it's definitely not going anywhere," Anakin said.

"We ran into a reclumi," Obi-Wan said.

"Web!" Dane shouted.

"Yes, a big one —"

"No, Web! That's his name! The assassin," Dane said. "I met him about two years ago. Robior Web. We had auditioned for the same job but he didn't get hired. The thing about him was, he got started as a security officer but the security force was disbanded on his planet so he found himself out of a job. He's got a reputation for taking on big jobs, assassinations, things like that. He used to be a Guardian on Junction 5."

Obi-Wan slowly rose.

"There is our connection to Lorian Nod," he said.

Promising to return, Obi-Wan and Anakin raced out of the prison and into the inn. They found Lorian in a secluded area of the lobby, deep in conference with the rulers of Bezim and Vicondor. Obi-Wan and Anakin hovered unseen, able to pick up some of their conversation.

"What is happening?" Yura Telamarch asked, his voice full of distress. The ruler of Bezim was a tall humanoid with a domed head and a grave manner. "Do you think Count Dooku is behind the murder of Kash?"

"I don't know, Yura," Lorian said. "They've arrested Samish's bodyguards. It could be an internal plot of Delaluna."

"We are not safe here," Glimmer Uziel, the ruler of Vicondor, said. She had a musical voice and pale gold skin. Four tiny tentacles waved delicately in the air, like fronds. "What if this is a trap? There are those among my aides who say that Count Dooku will not show up. He has lured us here to kill us all and take the space station by force."

"Without Samish, our alliance is weaker," Yura said. "No doubt the pressure will increase. What do you think, Lorian?"

"I think we trust Dooku for now," Lorian answered. He stood. "I suggest you get some rest. The meeting is scheduled to take place in an hour."

Reluctantly Yura and Glimmer rose and headed for the stairs. As soon as the rulers were out of sight, Obi-Wan and Anakin walked up to Lorian. "Trust Dooku?" Obi-Wan asked sardonically. "Good advice, Lorian."

"What did you expect me to say?" Lorian asked. "Dooku must not suspect that I am against him."

"Are you against him?" Obi-Wan asked. "Things have changed now that Samish Kash is dead. If someone wished to drive a wedge through the alliance, it has worked."

"Are you accusing me of killing Samish? He was my friend."

"So you say. Have you ever heard of Robior Web?" Obi-Wan asked.

Lorian frowned. "The name is familiar, but . . ."

"He was a Guardian."

"I could hardly be expected to remember every Guardian."

"He is now working as an assassin."

Lorian took several moments to reply. "He is on Null?"

"Yes. Dane recognized him."

Lorian nodded slowly. "You think this Web killed Kash, and I hired him to do it."

Obi-Wan said nothing.

"I did not," Lorian said. "And if you think about it for a

moment you will see that if someone wanted to smash the alliance, the way to do so would be to kill one member and pin the murder on another. It is no accident that the assassin is a former Guardian. Naturally you would suspect me."

"Naturally," Obi-Wan said.

"And that is exactly what Dooku would want Yura and Glimmer to do," Lorian continued. "This is how he works. He waits. He watches. He likes to undermine loyalties. He likes to fracture bonds. He likes to encourage betrayal."

All of this was true, but it didn't mean Lorian wasn't guilty. Just clever.

"There is more going on here than the Force can sense," Lorian said. "And more than your logic can decipher. There are feelings here, Obi-Wan. And among those feelings are mine for Samish. I did not do it."

"We have only your word for it, along with everything else," Obi-Wan said. "That is the problem."

"There is only one solution to the problem, then," Lorian said. "You must trust me."

"Can you give me any reason to do so?" Obi-Wan asked.

Lorian hesitated. "No. I cannot prove my honesty."

"Then we'll continue to suspect you," Anakin said.

"We come from the same place," Lorian said, looking at them both. "I was raised in the Temple. I fell away from its teachings for a time. Why? I was afraid. I was young and alone and I took a step forward, the only step I felt I could take. Then I took another, and another, and I ended up in a life I didn't recognize."

"These are excuses," Obi-Wan said. "Tell that to the people of Junction 5. Tell that to Cilia Dil."

"I harmed my people," Lorian admitted. "And I must say that Cilia is not one of my supporters. She can't forget what I was. I know all I have are excuses. When you live a life filled with wrong, what else do you have but excuses and blame?" He paused. "Do you believe in redemption, Obi-Wan?"

Obi-Wan had been asked the question, but it was Anakin who spoke up. "I do."

"I do, as well, young Anakin Skywalker," Lorian said. "It is what keeps me going. At the end of my life, I will do good. That's all I can tell you for now."

"Do you believe him?" Anakin asked as they walked outside the inn.

"I think he talks well," Obi-Wan said. "And I don't know what to believe. Not yet." Would Qui-Gon have known? He had always seemed to know who to trust.

"You are too hard on beings sometimes," Anakin said. "Mistakes are made. Things happen. That means that change can happen, too."

"The meaning of life *is* change," Obi-Wan said, startled at Anakin's characterization of him. The charge stung. He did not think he was hard on other beings. Perhaps that had been true once, but he had learned from Qui-Gon. "I didn't say I didn't believe Lorian. But I can't discount the rest of his life just because he tells me I should. If he is in league with Dooku, we should find out what they are planning. And if he is not in league with Dooku, we should still find out."

"So what's our next step?" Anakin asked.

"Do you have any suggestions?" Obi-Wan asked.

"I have a question," Anakin said. "If Robior Web was hired to kill Samish Kash, he has accomplished his objective. Why is he still on Null? Assassins seldom hang around after they finish an assignment."

"He was going to meet Lorian and give his report," Obi-Wan said.

"That could be true," Anakin said, "but usually that is done by comlink or dataport. Usually an assassin and his employer don't like to be seen together."

"So if he's still on Null, he could have another assignment to accomplish before the meeting," Obi-Wan said. "Maybe we should find him."

"Sure," Anakin said. "But how? It's a big mountain."

"Exactly," Obi-Wan said. "If I were Web, I'd want transport. His was destroyed. I'd need to do it without attracting any attention, so that lets out stealing one from a villager or an aide. But he knows where another one is —"

Anakin grinned and finished the sentence. "— just hanging around."

*　　*　　*

When they got to where Dane's speeder was hanging emeshed in the spiderweb, Robior Web was in the tree, trying to slice the web with his vibroblade. It was clear he had been trying for some time to release the swoop. His hands and tunic were covered with the sticky, ropy web. He had managed to free the back of the swoop, and it hung suspended from the handlebars, which were covered in the sticky goo. Below on the ground, a dead reclumi spider lay in pieces, a victim of the same vibroblade, no doubt when it tried to defend its web.

Robior Web consulted a chrono, then attacked the web even more fiercely. He succeeded only in winding a large tendril of the web around his arm. They could not hear his curses, but they could see his frustration.

"Time is running out," Obi-Wan murmured. "My guess is he has an appointment."

With one last savage thrust, Robior Web managed to cut loose a ropy tendril, but it flopped away, then smacked back against the body of the swoop. Now it was more enmeshed than ever.

With a strangled cry, the assassin dropped from the tree and hit the ground. He began to run.

Obi-Wan and Anakin followed. They had to keep well behind, but it was easy to track his progress through the forest. He was heading around the mountain but climbing steadily.

"I think he's heading for the landing platform," Obi-Wan said. "We'll be coming at it from above."

After a hard climb, they realized Obi-Wan was right. Robior Web climbed over a peak and disappeared below. Obi-Wan and Anakin waited a moment, then climbed behind him and peered over the edge. Web was moving down toward the landing platform below.

Suddenly the sun was blocked out overhead. They looked up. A large transport was hovering. Robior Web quickened his pace and almost slid down to the deserted landing platform.

Behind the large transport, a sleek interstellar sloop dropped down from the sky, a sail ship, like none other in the galaxy.

"Dooku has arrived," Obi-Wan said.

The solar sailer landed. The landing ramp slid down and the tall, elegant figure of Count Dooku emerged. Obi-Wan felt Anakin tense. Unconsciously, he touched the metal hand that had replaced the one Dooku had severed.

"So Dooku hired the assassin," Obi-Wan muttered as Robior Web skidded to a stop in front of Dooku, then bowed. "With or without Lorian, we don't know."

Distracted, he had not realized Anakin was rising until his Padawan was almost to his feet.

"Anakin what are you doing? Get down!"

"Let's get him now," Anakin said.

"Get down!" Obi-Wan insisted. To his relief, Anakin crouched down again. He faced him, his eyes full of fire and purpose.

"We have our chance to end it here," Anakin said. "Let's kill him. We can take him together. We won't make the same mistakes this time."

"Like being reckless and rushing him without a plan?" Obi-Wan asked pointedly. "It is what cost you your hand last time, and you are doing it again, Padawan."

"What are we waiting for?" Anakin asked. "We missed him at Raxus Prime, but we won't here. If we kill him, we kill the Separatist movement. What is one life against thousands? Maybe millions?"

"Anakin —"

"He killed our brothers and sisters on Geonosis," Anakin said bitterly. "Have you forgotten how they died?"

"I remember it every moment," Obi-Wan said. "But this is not the time. This is not the way."

"You don't know what I can do," Anakin said, and there was an ominous tone in his voice. "My connection to the Force is stronger than yours. I'm telling you I can do it! No matter what you say."

Obi-Wan was shocked. "You are still my apprentice," he said sharply. "I am your Master. You must obey."

The set of Anakin's mouth was sullen.

"Anakin, you must trust me," Obi-Wan said forcefully. "There will be another time to face Dooku. This is not the time."

Anakin looked at him. The sullen look was gone. His gaze was clear and cool. Obi-Wan could almost read contempt in it. But as the thought occurred to him, the look was gone. Had he really seen it?

"Look below," Obi-Wan said. "What do you think is in that transport? Super battle droids. We would be dead before we took two steps on that platform. They're being unloaded now."

Anakin looked down at the platform. Lines of droids clicked into formation as they rolled off the transport. Obi-Wan could see the way Anakin's mind focused on the immediate problem. He could almost feel Anakin's anger drain away.

But why had it been there in the first place? Obi-Wan had a feeling he had seen a flash of something much deeper than he'd ever known before.

"He is taking no chances," Obi-Wan guessed. "If things do not go his way at the meeting, he will use force."

Reluctantly, Anakin tore his gaze away. "We should warn them."

"Yes," Obi-Wan said. "But who? Any one of them could be secretly in league with Dooku. We must consider our next step carefully. We must figure out who to talk to first."

"I say we talk to Floria," Anakin said.

"Why Floria?" Obi-Wan asked, puzzled. He didn't know what Anakin was thinking. He rarely did, anymore. But at least he was glad they were talking.

"I sense she is not telling all she knows," Anakin said.

Obi-Wan thought back. He realized that he had picked

up something from Floria, too. But he had been too focused on Lorian to consider it.

Your mind must be everywhere at once, Padawan. The truth has many sides.

Yes, Qui-Gon.

"There is more going on here than the Force can sense," Anakin said, repeating Lorian's words. "*Feelings,* he said. What did he mean?"

"I don't know," Obi-Wan said.

"That is why we must talk to Floria," Anakin said. He rose to his feet in one quick movement and began to run. Obi-Wan had to put on a burst of speed to catch up.

"Do you remember," Anakin said, "how upset she was when the body of Samish Kash was found?"

"She had failed in her mission to protect him," Obi-Wan said.

"I think the loss was more personal," Anakin said. "And later she called him 'Samish.' Dane always calls him 'Kash.' I think she's in love with him."

"How is that relevant to our mission?"

Anakin shot him a sidelong look. Amazing that they were running hard down a mountain, and Anakin could still have the energy for a healthy dose of scorn.

"Love is always relevant, Master," he said.

CHAPTER No. **25**

Another bribe got them access to the cell.

"Take your time," the villager said, waving a hand as the door slid open. "We've decided to kill them at dawn."

The rest of the villagers roared and pounded the table. They had been drinking grog for some time now. The door slid shut, drowning out their laughter.

"Did you hear that?" Dane hissed at Floria.

"She's not afraid," Anakin said. "Why is that, Floria?"

"I am not panicking like my brother, it's true," Floria said.

"And you are no longer grieving," Anakin said. "Why is that?"

Floria turned her extraordinary sky-blue eyes on Anakin. They looked at each other for a long moment.

"You love him," Anakin said.

"Of course she loves me," Dane said. "I'm her brother."

Another long silence. Anakin waited her out. Obi-Wan kept very still.

"I love Samish," Floria admitted. Her chin lifted and her eyes flashed, as though to say the words out loud had given her great pleasure.

"You love who?" Dane shouted.

"And he is still alive," Anakin said.

Floria nodded.

"What?" Dane cried, leaping in front of Floria. "You love Samish Kash, and he's still alive?"

"Dane, stop. He was shot, but he survived," Floria said. "He decided to let everyone think he was dead after the attempt on his life. He wanted to find out who had put a price on his head and why. The alliance is very important to him, and he doesn't trust Dooku."

"He was our employer!" Dane said. "We worked for him. You were his bodyguard. You went against all professional standards —"

"Be quiet," Anakin ordered, turning on Dane. "Floria couldn't help her feelings."

"You can always help your feelings," Dane said. "Feelings *need* help. Otherwise they get completely out of control!"

Obi-Wan ignored Dane. "When we first saw you, you thought Samish Kash was dead." At Floria's nod, he continued. "How did you find out he was alive?"

"You let me think I was going to be executed!" Dane cried, as a fresh wave of indignation swept over him.

"Lorian told me," Floria said. "He had brought Kash to the clinic. He, too, had thought he was dead. Kash revived on the med table. Lorian bribed the doctor and he and Samish came up with the plan. The first thing Samish asked Lorian to do was tell me. Right after that, we were arrested."

"Did you ever think of mentioning that the person we supposedly killed wasn't dead?" Dane asked.

"I couldn't say anything. Not until the meeting," Floria said. "If Dooku has a plan, it will take place there. Lorian and Samish decided that Samish should show up at the meeting. If Dooku had arranged his assassination, it might be enough to foil his plans."

"So Lorian told the truth," Obi-Wan said. "He didn't hire the assassin. He could have gotten off the hook by telling us Samish was alive, and he didn't."

"He had sworn to keep the secret," Floria said. "Samish always said Lorian had come both early and late to honor. I wasn't sure what he meant."

"I think I do." Obi-Wan looked at Anakin. "They are walking into a trap," he said.

A trap he could have prevented. He could have told Lorian about the battle droids, and he had not. Angry with himself, Obi-Wan piloted the speeder up the mountain toward Dooku's villa at maximum speed. It had only taken a little truth, a little persuasion, and two glowing lightsabers to get the villagers to release their prisoners. As soon as they heard that Samish Kash was alive and that the two hunters were actually Jedi, they even turned over several speeders for their use.

Obi-Wan and Anakin had each taken a speeder. Floria and Dane insisted on coming with them. Despite everything, Dane considered Samish Kash his responsibility to protect. Floria just wanted to be with him, "whatever happens."

The villa rose above them, as gray and forbidding as the stone mountain. The meeting was about to begin. Obi-Wan saw the security gate ahead. The speeder had light armor mounted on the hull. He opened fire and blasted his way through the gate. Immediately a durasteel shield began to descend over the wide double doors of the front entrance. It would no doubt prove impenetrable to explosives.

Before Obi-Wan could react, Anakin gunned his speeder, blasting his weaponry at the double doors beyond the descending shield. In an amazing display of skill, he cut the power, flipping his speeder up at the same time and leaping off. The speeder skidded to a stop, its armored hull pointing up toward the swiftly descending shield.

The shield came down on the speeder. Metal shrieked and groaned, slowing the descent of the shield. Anakin ducked under the moving shield and leaped through the hole he had blasted through the double doors. He disappeared into the darkness of the villa.

This had all taken only seconds. Obi-Wan had already leaped off his speeder and was running toward the durasteel shield, now slowly crushing the speeder underneath it. There was just enough room for Obi-Wan to duck underneath and inside. Floria and Dane followed, rolling under the door as it goaned downward and shut with a crash, the speeder now part pancake, part mangled transport.

Anakin was waiting in the darkness of the hallway. The ceiling was so high it was lost in the gloom above. Together they ran down the grand hall, looking into the large rooms as they passed. They heard voices ahead.

Obi-Wan slipped into a circular room that had been built in the center of the villa. There was no ceiling, only the roof above. Narrow windows were cut into the stone high above and let in a faint light. One entire wall was made up of an enormous fireplace, big enough for a Null to stand erect in. A large circular stone table sat in the center of the room, but it was dwarfed by the soaring space. Dooku stood at one end. Samish stood at the opposite side of the table, facing him. Yura, Glimmer, and Lorian looked small and defenseless. The table was so large that there was an expanse of space between each of them.

Obi-Wan guessed that Dooku had sensed his presence. He felt the dark side in the room, how it surged and grew. Anakin came and stood next to him, and Floria and Dane followed, staying against the wall in the shadows so that they would not be seen.

"I believe you tried to assassinate me so you could smash the alliance," Samish was saying.

"So much emotion, so little logic," Dooku said. "Let us be calm. Station 88 Spaceport is a vital strategic link. This is something that must be decided carefully. You have not even heard what my organization is willing to give to you for the rights to the spaceport. I am sure your partners would want to hear. Do you deny them that right?"

Samish looked uncertain. "Yes, we should at least hear him out," Yura said.

Anakin stirred. Obi-Wan put a hand on his arm. If they moved, Dooku was capable of anything. And he had seen Robior Web standing against the wall, almost lost in the shadows. He had no doubt that Samish Kash was in danger, and most likely all of the other rulers in the alliance, as well.

Samish turned to the others. "Why should we listen? Everything he is about to tell us will be lies."

Dooku turned to Lorian. "We haven't heard from you, old friend. Tell Samish what you have decided."

Lorian stood. "I support Samish Kash. And I support the Republic."

Dooku gripped the edge of the table. It was clear that a great surge of rage had overtaken him. He controlled it. His dark eyes seemed to suck in the light around the table and devour it.

He leaned over the table. "So you betray me again. I assure you, it is for the last time, Lorian."

"Yes," Lorian said. "I am certain of that."

"Vicondor must stand with Delaluna and Junction 5, my friends Samish and Lorian," Glimmer said. "The alliance will support the Republic."

Dooku looked over into the shadows and acknowledged the Jedi for the first time. "So you support a corrupt government?" he thundered. "Have you forgotten the battle of Geonosis, how they crushed a small planet with an invading army? They are ruthless. They hide in the shadows. Look!"

The rulers turned and saw the Jedi. Lorian appeared very glad to see them. "That is one way of looking at it," he said. "But it is not the truth."

"I stand with the decision of the alliance," Yura said.

"It appears the negotiation is over," Dooku said. He had controlled his anger and spoke now in a mild tone. "How unfortunate. I suppose I could try to persuade you. But as I grow older, I have found that I have so little . . . patience for such things."

The door behind Obi-Wan, Anakin, Floria, and Dane slid shut. They heard the security locks snap. Shutters slid down over the windows and the room was thrown into deep shadow.

Then hidden doors in the walls of the circular room slid open and at least a dozen super battle droids marched in.

Obi-Wan saw it all happen in a frozen moment. There was Dooku. There were the droids. There was Robior Web, the capable assassin.

Yura, Glimmer, and Kash were not fighters, but politicians. Floria and Dane could handle themselves, but not against such firepower. There were too many beings to protect. And it was clear that Dooku meant to murder them all. The room was a trap. It was a tomb.

He remembered the arena at Geonosis, the arrival of the gunships, the battle, the slaughter.

In that frozen moment the thought blazed, white-hot and searing: *I cannot bear one more death.* It was illogical — he knew in his heart that he would have to bear many more — but not today.

Not today.

Dooku stepped back from the table. Anakin charged, putting himself between the approaching droids and the politicians. Fire erupted from the super battle droids at the same time. Yura and Glimmer both sensibly dropped to the floor.

No one had expected Floria to move so fast.

She streaked across the space as Obi-Wan was moving to deflect the blaster fire of the droids. She would come between Dooku and Anakin, a dangerous place to be.

Single-minded, intent, Anakin increased his speed. Obi-Wan saw him move from light to shadow, shadow to light. He felt the Force in the room like a pulse, like a heartbeat, like a rolling wave.

"Anakin, Floria!" he shouted.

Anakin shuddered with the effort of stopping his relentless charge. He altered his path to scoop up Floria, tucked her under his arm, and kept his lightsaber moving, deflecting the blaster fire of the droids. He deposited Floria next to Samish Kash, so lightly and gently in the midst of his soaring leap that not even a hair of Floria's coiled braids was disturbed.

Obi-Wan saw the relief on the face of Samish Kash. Anakin had been right about Floria's love. Now Obi-Wan saw the same love on Samish's face. He would not allow these two to die.

He caught the surging Force from Anakin and embraced it, doubling it, making it grow. The droids reconverged on the rulers. Obviously they were programmed to target them. Anakin leaped again, and Obi-Wan met him in midair. They swept the room in a glance. There were only seconds to decide on a strategy.

Dooku was leaving. They saw his cloak flicker as he moved toward the wall, toward the one door that still stood open.

Lorian saw Dooku moving and ran toward him.

Yura and Glimmer had no weapons. They sat, back-to-back behind a massive chair for protection that was being rapidly decimated by the droid blasts. The expression on their faces told Obi-Wan that they were waiting for death and would meet it bravely.

Floria handed one blaster to Samish and had the other in her hand. While Samish and Dane tried to protect her, she shot a droid repeatedly with unerring accuracy. It flamed out and fell heavily on the table.

Robior Web took aim at Samish.

Obi-Wan landed, then jumped again, somersaulting in midair and landing against Web's chest with both feet. The assassin flew back and hit a chunk of stone protruding from the wall. He lay still.

Obi-Wan had time to register the chunk of stone with only a flash of his consciousness, but something about it was important. He was busy deflecting blaster fire as it pinged past him toward Yura and Glimmer.

Anakin had managed to herd the group together in one corner of the room so that they would be easier to protect. With a swipe of his lightsaber, he hewed off a chunk of the stone table, then pushed the others behind it for protection.

They could only last so long, Obi-Wan thought desperately. They could not win against these droids.

The chunk of stone — why did it keep rising in his mind?

The keystone. One pull of the keystone and the whole wall comes tumbling down.

Obi-Wan raced back to Anakin. They spoke while they protected the others, deflecting fire. Samish, Dane, and Floria popped out to fire at the droids, then dived for cover again.

"Glimmer has been hit in the leg," Anakin said. "Lorian went after Dooku. We have to help him. We have to get out of here."

"The keystone in the fireplace," Obi-Wan said. "If we herd the others to the opposite end of the room quickly, then pull the keystone, it would knock out most of the droids."

Anakin's eyes traveled over the fireplace wall even as his lightsaber whirled.

"Finding it, of course, is the problem," Obi-Wan said.

He felt Anakin gather in the Force then, feeling it shimmer from the stones and the wood and the living beings, feeling it grow . . . Anakin focused on the wall.

Obi-Wan saw one stone midway up the wall ease out a fraction. He heard a rumble.

"Move!" he shouted, leaping toward the others. He picked up Glimmer, pushed Yura, yelled in Samish's ear, "Go to the doorway!"

They moved, ran, scrambled, as the wall began to move and the rumbling and scraping filled the air. Then the rocks shot forward, tumbling in a lethal avalanche, spewing dust and debris far taller than any person. The rocks and part of the ceiling tumbled on the droids, sending them careening into walls, the floor, and one another.

Obi-Wan and Anakin pushed the others down and tried to cover them with their bodies as the wall collapsed. The dust and smoke bit into their lungs and stung their eyes. They could taste the mountain in their mouths.

But they were all alive.

Three droids were still standing. Obi-Wan and Anakin ran, covered in dust, and brought them down.

Then they faced the pile of rubble. Behind it was the doorway where Count Dooku had disappeared and where Lorian had followed. It would take some time to get out of the collapsed chamber.

"May the Force be with him," Obi-Wan said.

CHAPTER No. **26**

Lorian had not felt the Force in many years. When he reached out and felt it move, it startled him, as if he'd burned his hand.

But within seconds, it all rushed back, and he knew he could depend on it.

Dooku was ahead of him in the narrow passageway, running toward an airspeeder. Dooku must have known very well that Lorian was behind him, but he didn't bother to turn and engage him. Lorian was sure that Dooku was taking no more notice of him than he would a fly.

He had no time to think of strategy. He knew Dooku was vastly more powerful. Why was he doing this? he thought as he ran. Why? It was a death wish, a fool's errand, and he had never courted death or been a fool.

All the wrongs of his life, all the mistakes, all the un forgivable deeds, all the pain he had caused, all the lives he had broken, they were all here in this dark corridor. They would choke him, they would lay him flat, but the Force had touched him just when he needed it, bringing a memory of a childhood when he knew what was right and wanted to do it.

He had a blaster, but he knew its puny power would mean nothing to Dooku. Within seconds it would be wrenched from his grasp and fly across the corridor.

So why use it? Why use any weapon when Dooku could swat it away like a fly?

Lorian had not stopped running while he thought. What did he have that Dooku did not have? What did he know about Dooku that no one else knew? What did he know about him as a boy that would not have changed? Did he have a flaw?

Pride. He was vain. He liked to be admired.

That wasn't much to go on.

Then Lorian noticed the airspeeder at the end of the corridor, ahead of Dooku. He was familiar with the model. It was a Mobquet twin turbojet with a boosted max airspeed. Mobquet Industries were known for their swoop bikes, not their speeders. Dooku's transport was a good choice for quick getaways, with its boosted airspeed and high maneuverability. But possibly, just possibly, Dooku did not know this: The Mobquet speeder had a flaw. The data cables that connected the frontal controls to the cabin were mounted behind a thin panel on the underside of the body. It would take Lorian about six seconds to find that panel and fuse those cables with a barrage from his blaster.

All he needed was six seconds.

He called ahead, his voice echoing. "You've done well for yourself, Dooku. But did you ever realize that you couldn't have done it without me?"

Dooku stopped and turned, as Lorian had known he would.

"Excuse me, old friend?"

"The Sith Holocron. You accessed it, didn't you? Sometime later. You could never stand it if I knew something you didn't."

"Why shouldn't I have accessed it?" Dooku asked.

Lorian kept moving forward. "Of course you had the right. Yet you never would have had the courage if I hadn't done it first."

Dooku laughed. "You are unbelievable. Don't you realize how tempted I am to kill you? And now you're provoking me. You certainly live dangerously, Lorian."

Lorian had circled around Dooku and stood near the speeder. Dooku was not afraid of him; he would allow him to come as close as he wanted. Lorian leaned against the speeder, crossing his leg as though he had all the time in the world to chat. "I realize now that I was wrong when I asked you to cover for me about the Holocron."

"An apology at this late date? I'm overwhelmed."

"I should have taken the responsibility myself. I wouldn't have been kicked out of the Jedi Order. I see that now. But now I wonder . . . why did I think I would?" Underneath the cover of his cloak, Lorian's fingers searched for the panel.

"I find revisiting the past so tedious," Dooku said. "If you'll excuse me —"

He put one foot on the speeder, ready to leap inside.

"Could it be that you encouraged my fears? Looking back, I find that strange. I would not have done that to you. I would not have fed your fears, but tried to allay them." His fingers slid across a seam. He had found the panel.

Dooku's eyes flared. Lorian brought out the blaster and put the barrel against the panel.

The dark side surged in a shocking display of power, and Lorian found himself flung like a child's doll in the air. He slammed against the wall and then hit the floor, dazed. Somehow, he held on to his blaster.

Dooku saw it, of course. "That was your clumsy attempt at a diversion, I suppose," he said, drawing his lightsaber with the curved hilt. "I think I've shown enough mercy. Let us end now what should have ended then."

He had one last chance. One only. He could blast the panel and prevent Dooku from taking off. Obi-Wan and Anakin would have to do the rest. If he failed, he would die. If he succeeded, he would also die. He had no doubt about that.

Lorian reached out to the Force to help him. He needed it here, at the last. He felt it grow, and he saw Dooku's eyebrows rise.

"So you haven't lost it completely," he said. "Too bad it isn't enough."

He moved toward Lorian. Lorian remembered his footwork. The attack would come to his left. At the last moment, he rolled to the right, and Dooku's lightsaber hit rock and sliced through it. Expecting an easy blow, Dooku turned a second too late, and Lorian had already begun to run. He knew Dooku expected him to turn and try to get behind him. He would not expect him to run to the speeder.

He had the blaster aimed and ready, but he knew he would get only one shot, and it had to be a good one. It had to be dead solid perfect —

Behind him was a whisper. That was all he heard. He looked down and saw the lightsaber and he thought, how odd, Dooku is behind me, why is the lightsaber in front of me? Then he realized he had been pierced through.

He fired the blaster, but the shot went wild. He went down.

I have failed, he thought. *I have failed.*

Dooku stood over him. He saw the dark eyes like hollow caves. He did not want this to be his last sight. He had lived so long with hate, he could not die with it in his vision. So with a great effort, he turned his head. He saw the rocks of the corridor, the stones both smooth and jagged, and noticed for the first time that they weren't gray, but were veined with silver and black and red and a blue the color of stars. . . .

The thought pierced him with the same sure pain as the lightsaber had: *What else have I missed?*

Too late to find out now.

He drew the Force around him like a blanket, and with an explosion of color lighting his vision, he smiled and let go of his life.

Anakin sat on the cold ground, watching the streaks of orange cut through the gray. The sun was rising.

"It is time to go," Obi-Wan said.

Anakin rose. He was tired after having moved the hundreds of large stones that had barred their exit.

"I've brought Lorian's body aboard," Obi-Wan said. He stood next to Anakin, facing the rising sun. "We will take him back to the Temple."

They had found him in the corridor with a blaster nearby, his eyes open and, oddly, a faint smile on his face. There was evidence of a struggle in the disturbance in the dirt. Blaster fire had marked the rocks. They could see the acceleration blast marks from a speeder. Dooku had escaped.

"Lorian went up against impossible odds," Obi-Wan said. "He was never more a Jedi than at the last."

"So redemption is possible," Anakin said.

"Of course it is," Obi-Wan said. "As long as there is breath, there is hope. If not, what are we fighting for?"

"I wish I didn't feel that I had failed," Anakin said. "Dooku escaped. The Station 88 Spaceport is saved for the Republic, but for how long? What is to stop Dooku from trying to kill them again?"

"We are," Obi-Wan said.

"There is such darkness ahead," Anakin said. He stopped outside the cruiser and looked up at the stars. They were fading in the growing light. "I can feel it. It weighs on me."

You worry too much. Qui-Gon had told Obi-Wan this, more than once. Was that his legacy to Anakin? He had tried to give him so much more.

"You didn't fail here, Anakin," Obi-Wan said. "Our mission was to ensure that the spaceport didn't fall to the Separatists, and to gather information. We succeeded. Dooku's villa contains valuable data."

"A small victory," Anakin said with a curl of his lip. "Can we win a war that way?"

He had not reached him. Anakin had wanted to end the Clone Wars here. He had wanted to destroy Count Dooku. His ambition would always be greater than every mission. Obi-Wan saw that clearly, and it pierced him. He had taught Anakin everything, and Anakin had learned much — but had he missed the most important things?

I have failed, Qui-Gon. I have failed.

They walked up the landing ramp. Anakin slid behind the controls. Obi-Wan sat at the computer to enter the co-ordinates for their journey back. On the surface, everything was as it had always been.

Soon they would be ending their journey together.

They both knew it. He had never had to bid good-bye to Qui-Gon as a Master. He was still Qui-Gon's Padawan when he died. Maybe that was the reason he felt so close to him still.

He did not know if Qui-Gon would have left him with words of wisdom, with a direction to follow. Now he had no way of knowing what else he could give Anakin. He had given him everything he could. It wasn't enough.

Sadness filled Obi-Wan as they blasted into the upper atmosphere. He loved Anakin Skywalker, but he did not truly know him. The most important things he had to teach he had not taught. He would have to let him go, knowing that. He would have to let him go.